Encountering the Monster

Encountering the Monster

Pathways in Children's Dreams

Denyse Beaudet
Foreword by Robert A. Johnson

CONTINUUM • NEW YORK

1990

The Continuum Publishing Company
370 Lexington Avenue, New York, N.Y. 10017

Printed in the United States of America

Library of Congress Cataloging-in-Publication Data

Beaudet, Denyse.
    Encountering the monster: pathways in children's dreams / Denyse
Beaudet; foreword by Robert A. Johnson.
        p.   cm.
    Includes bibliographical references.
    ISBN 0-8264-0460-X
    1. Children's dreams.   I. Title.
BF1099.C55B43   1990
154.6'3'083—dc20   89-28706
                                                                         CIP

Grateful acknowledgment is made to Yale University Press for permission to
reprint Diagram 3 on page 87 of *The Psychology of C. G. Jung*, by Jolande Jacobi,
translated by Ralph Mannheim, © 1962, 1968, 1973 Jolande Jacobi; here
reprinted as Figure 6 on page 36.

To Mikhaëla
and to all child-dreamers

Contents

List of Tables

Foreword

Denyse Beaudet's exploration of the dreams of children, and in particular her exploration of how children encounter the monster, shows that the unconscious plays a vital role in child development. The ingenuity of her approach lies in its simplicity, but its implications for understanding the dream life of children are rich and varied. Parents, teachers, researchers, and therapists may all benefit from her findings and from using elements of her approach. Most of all, children may benefit from her approach, for within it lie potent and respectful attitudes toward their inner lives, attitudes which promote a dialogue between the personality and the unconscious.

It surprises us to find such deep layers of human life in people so young, because we do not expect the weight, creativity, and symbolic power of the unconscious to be so fully present in the lives of children. But the split in our psyche between consciousness and that vast instinctive life from which we are so estranged begins in childhood, and healing it may begin in childhood also. To our present understanding of child development we must now add the unconscious dimension of that development and also the development of the child's relationship to the unconscious, since both have come into view in this work.

Like the outer planet that was predicted in theory long before it was sighted, we might have expected to find that the child's unconscious would communicate its development in dreams and that a child not specially trained in "the art of dreaming" could participate. But now we have empirical confirmation. We do not have a complete map, but we have unmistakable signs of a continuity with adolescent and adult development, and continuity with the human legacy left us in myth and fairy tale. Erich Neumann and Joseph Campbell in particular would be delighted to have this confirmation. Beyond the richness and depth in children's dreams noted by Carl Jung, Frances Wickes, and many others, it now appears that the child, like the adult, can receive dreams that, if viewed in a series, have larger developmental trajectories. Viewing the monster found in these series from young children as an initiator suggests that the unconscious is goal-oriented, and not simply preoccupied with images concerned with past traumas and present wishes.

Encountering the Monster: Pathways in Children's Dreams is not tangled up in technical methods that quantify children's dreams or manipulate them for proving a point. Instead, it lays before us the dreams themselves in their series, and brings to them a method, amplification, that helps access their larger meanings. The experience is one of a journey into greater and more precise meanings. If we want to understand the lives of children in their fullness, the encounter with the monster in their dreams must not be left out of account. And if children can be understood in this dimension of their lives, their search for knowing themselves is supported early in their lives. There are few gifts greater than this support that we can give.

The food for the life of the unconscious that children are given these days seems to have very little that is nourishing in it. Cartoons, advertising jingles aimed at inducing material desires, schooling focused on cognitive manipulation of words and numbers, and family lives captive to juggling over-stuffed schedules of outer events do not feed the inner life with its own real food. There does not seem to be much time and value given to the activity that Walt Whitman described when he wrote, "I loaf and invite my soul." The timeless stories of essential human predicaments and how we change to meet them seem to live now only in the unconscious. But they do live there. This book draws our attention to the enduring struggles underneath the ephemeral. And the course of action it describes, embodies, and recommends has the nourishment that seems so lacking.

Robert A. Johnson

Acknowledgments

Several people have been significant allies on the way through this study and in the writing of this book. I am grateful to them. David DeBus co-translated this book with me from the French and contributed his fine gift with words. Robert A. Johnson graciously accepted writing the Foreword. And Christine Downing grasped the spirit of this work and made invaluable suggestions for its editing.

André Paré's understanding of research and his faith in the creative process made possible the necessary descent to the source from which I could return with a fresh perspective on the dreams received from children. Thérèse Laferrière brought her expertise with research to my project. Others collaborated: Bibiane d'Anjou, Françoise Loranger, Roland Bourneuf.

The teacher in whose classroom I conducted this study welcomed me and brought to my enterprise her open-minded sensitivity. I am grateful to her. To the children who shared their dreams with such candor, and in particular to Eric, Pierre, and Marjorie, whose dreams taught me so much, I owe thanks beyond words.

Friends, colleagues, sometimes perfect strangers, have also generously shared their childhood dreams with me, or shared their experience as parents of dreaming children.

Finally, I want to acknowledge the responsive and competent cooperation of Frank Oveis, my editor at Crossroad/Continuum.

Introduction

Night is an immensity from which dreams emerge, some like shadows and some like piercing rays of light. This book offers an approach to dreams, the dreams of children. It follows the encounter with the monster in the dream life of children, and the meaning of that encounter for their psychological development. It is addressed to dreamers of all ages: to parents, educators, and therapists; to researchers and students. It concerns all who are interested in education about dreams, in the symbolic life, in the tasks needed for growing up and the myths expressing those tasks, and it concerns everyone who is interested in childhood and the recognition of childhood.

My discovery of the educational practice of the Malaysian Senoi is at the origin of this study of children's dreams. The Senoi teach children very early in life to adopt an actively confronting and adventurous attitude toward challenges in their dreams. The anthropologist Herbert (Pat) Noone first called the attention of the Western world to the Senoi educational practice.

The Senoi live distant from cities, in the mountains of central Malaysia, where the jungle is very dense.[1] And to this day their territory is accessible only by boat or helicopter. The Senoi way of life revolves around an extended family. Traditionally they sleep in longhouses made of bamboo and mounted on stilts, inside of which each family has separate quarters. These longhouses are built to last from five to six years, as long as the soil is fertile there, and then the community moves to a new place.

Noone observed in the early 1930s that the Senoi reached a remarkable level of maturity and adaptation. He described them as a nonviolent and democratic people who were self-sufficient. Intercommunal conflict did not exist. The Senoi lived in great harmony with nature and they cooperated with one another. Noone attributed this state of affairs to the educational methods of the Senoi, and specifically to their way of working with dreams.[2]

1

For the Senoi, dreams are a spiritual experience as important and real as the sense experience of waking life. The Senoi take inspiration from their dreams for making decisions on how to govern their individual and collective life. Their dream life is also a source of creative inspiration: poems, songs, dances, music, mechanical inventions, decorations, and remedies come from their dreams.

Behind their model of dreaming, the Senoi have an animistic conception of the world. They hold that the "spirits" that show themselves in dreams as hostile images can become allies of the dreamer, but only if the dreamer has the courage to confront these images instead of fleeing them. The dream images that are not thus mastered, however, will torment the dreamer until he or she vanquishes them.

As a consequence, the Senoi adult teaches the child to be audacious with the monsters, animals, and ghosts met in dreams. The child is taught, for instance, that the tiger in a dream is not dangerous like the tiger in the jungle and that it must be fought. The adult persists in teaching this approach and attitude until both child and adult are convinced that the child has mastered the dream image of the tiger. After this mastery, the tiger is helpful rather than harmful to the child's interests.

As soon as children learn how to speak, they are invited to tell dreams, like the other family members. Children are questioned about their behavior during the dream and advised for future dreams. In order to dream adequately, the child must never be afraid. If the child reports a dream of falling, the adult exclaims, "Magnificent! This is the most beautiful dream that you can have. Where did you fall? What have you discovered?" If the child reports being afraid during this dream, and awakens before arriving somewhere, the adult tells the child that this is a mistake. The adult teaches the child that what is done in a dream has a goal beyond the child's understanding. The child is advised to relax and enjoy the movement of falling in the dream, since falling is the quickest way to make contact with the world of spirits and its powers. The adult knows that after a while the child's fear of falling will change into the joy of flying.

The Senoi child is trained to continue dreaming to the point of resolution, and to act in a responsible manner toward friends and other recognizable people seen in dreams. If the child is the victim of aggression from a friend during a dream, the child should tell the friend about it in waking life and give that friend the opportunity to repair the damage to her or his image. If the child attacks a friend in the dream, the child is invited to make amiable overtures and amends to the friend in waking life. But if the child witnesses aggression in a dream perpetrated against a friend, the child should warn the friend in waking life and come to the friend's defense during later dreams by fighting the aggressor.

A little later in childhood, an adult teaches the child to bring something beautiful or useful from dreams such as a poem, a chant, a dance, which the child may share with other members of the tribe. The dreams of the child evolve as the child grows older. When Senoi children reach adolescence, they know how to control their dreams. The Senoi consider one to be a full woman or man when the forces and beings in one's dreams cooperate with and serve one in living a creative and socially responsible life. After attaining adulthood, advanced training in dreaming is given the one who is called to become a *halak*, or medicine man.[3]

The Senoi practice is rooted in an ancient shamanic tradition. But we may ask how children in modern societies fare in their oneiric (dream) worlds when they do not receive such education in "the art of dreaming." This question has been the starting point for my study on children's dreams. For eleven weeks I collected the dreams of fifteen children between the ages of five and six in a preschool classroom close to Québec City in the Canadian province of Québec. At the end of my stay, I found myself with some one hundred dreams. Among these there were complete dreams, what seemed like dream fragments, dreams that developed as children drew them, what seemed like images fed by nocturnal fears, and simple fantasies.

At first glance, the symbolic material that the children had entrusted to me seemed scattered, diverse, and incoherent, and yet it also seemed fertile and rich with the imaginative life of children. I began by putting the dreams into different groups, observing their contents, their major themes, the settings in which they occurred, and the attitudes of the dreamers as they faced the challenges that they encountered in their dreams. The dreams pointed toward the monster. Sometimes the monster took the form of a phantasmagorical being, sometimes the form of an animal, and sometimes the form of a human being. I became interested in the dynamic relation between child and monster, and in the strategies to which the dreamers had recourse in coping with the monster in their dreams.

The children seemed to cope with encountering the monster by strategies that followed basic pathways: combat, taming, and being engulfed. Amplifying three series of dreams, one for each pathway, deepened my understanding of these pathways. Each pathway illuminated one facet of the nature of the monster, and also illuminated one task that the growing child needs to accomplish.

Chapter One

Listening to the Dreamers

There is such a wealth of imagery and such a frequent beauty of details in the child's dream that we cannot doubt that in the unconscious lies stored up for him a vast accumulation of that precious material from which poetry and painting have been born. Very interesting work remains to be done in helping the child to make use of the myth-making material which lies within himself. (Wickes 1978, 244)

T he dream life of young children has a wealth and depth most of us never suspected. To begin our approach to this wealth and depth, listening to the child-dreamers comes first. To listen requires that we give time and space to them in our lives. It requires that we cultivate our capacity to quiet ourselves inwardly, so that we become receptive to their dream experience.

I interviewed children in a preschool they attended. I established conditions under which I could be with the children on a day-to-day basis and wait for the dreams as the children brought them.[1] The dreams I studied came from fifteen children, seven girls and eight boys, in a preschool class in Ste.-Foy, a Québec City suburb. The children's ages ranged from five years and eight months to six years and five months, with the average five years and ten months.[2]

My objective was to collect dreams in the context most closely adapted to the daily life of the children and least likely to interfere with the spontaneous course of each child's psychic life. The school context, by contrast to the home or laboratory context, seemed the most appropriate for accomplishing this objective, since the children were already accustomed to having visitors, student teachers, supervisors, and parents in their classroom. I could insert myself naturally into this milieu.

Both the home interview and the electrophysiological laboratory method have advantages for studying children's dreams; but the drawbacks, by contrast to the school context, seemed greater. The home interview permits collecting dreams at the moment the child awakens, but it also requires the collaboration and training of parents, resulting in different interviewers and settings for each child. The laboratory method is characterized by technical rigor in procedure. But this method gives access only to one layer of a child's dream experience. It allows the researcher to collect dreams after waking up the child during rapid-eye-movement (REM) periods of sleep, gathering those dreams or fragments that typically occupy the child's mind while asleep. The child would normally remain unconscious of most of these dreams, since their energy is not sufficient to break through the child's sleep and impact the child's consciousness.

I was interested in those dreams that impose themselves on the child's consciousness, captivate the child's imagination, and express ongoing psychic processes that no language could better express. The laboratory method is not the best method for accessing this layer of the child's dream experience. Furthermore, confabulation, one of the most critical problems for the study of children's dreams, is not controlled by using a laboratory method. A child confabulates spontaneously, making up and adding bits and pieces and even episodes to the dream itself; and whether a laboratory or a clinical method is used, the child's nature and mind remain what they are.[3]

The school context allowed an integrated approach to the child's daily life. It permitted the attitude of waiting, and of being present long enough so the child's dream experience could be witnessed. The school context also allowed access to dreams while they were still "live" and active in the consciousness of the child.

The purpose of interviews in the school context was to explore the dreams of children with the collaboration of the children themselves, starting with their own experience and with their willingness to share it with me as a researcher. The design of the interview included the arrangement of the interview setting, the adoption of a rhythm of work, the selection of the procedures that would constitute an interview ritual, and beyond these, the cultivation of a quality of presence and listening that would help insure contact between the children and me.[4]

I had at my disposal a preschool classroom adjacent to the children's classroom, a tape recorder, colored felt-tipped pens, and seven children's storybooks on the subject of dreams. I had organized a corner with cushions for sitting on the floor, and a small table with two chairs for working with the children.

Children who wanted to paint their dream instead of drawing it could use the easels in the classroom, which were readily available for painting.

The interviews occurred during the last three months of the school year, between April 6 and June 21 (inclusive). I took three days to get acquainted with the group of children before beginning the interviews. Then I informed the children of my interest in dreams and of my intention to conduct a study of the dreams of children.

The first interview took place in small groups of three or four children. This group situation functioned as one of transition into the individual work that we were going to do. It also bore features of an educational rather than a clinical situation. This was closer to the spirit with which I wanted to start the research, and closer to the tone I wanted to impart to the enterprise.

The objective of this first interview in small groups was to raise directly with the children the questions of dreams in their lives. The subject of dreams was introduced by means of a child's story revolving around dreams. At the end of the story, I asked the children if they sometimes dreamed and what they dreamed about. For some of the children, the question had the effect of unleashing feelings and bringing forth a recollection of traumatic dreams. Many children recalled a dream, whereas others acknowledged dreaming but did not remember any specific dreams just then. The children who remembered a dream told their dream in the group, and then they drew or painted their dream. The other children made a drawing or a painting. When the children finished their work, we gathered again to look at the drawings and paintings. There were a few signs of children influencing one another. I noted four such instances, to which I shall later return (see the section "Centering on Three Strategies" in Chapter 3).

The subsequent interviews were individual ones. The children reported from between one and fourteen dreams each. When children had had a dream, I always gave them priority and interviewed them the day of their dream. But I also regularly interviewed all of the children, in order to avoid their feeling excluded from the study or compelled to invent dreams in order to visit me.

All the children came at least ten times for interviews. These sessions lasted from ten to forty minutes, depending on the material brought by the child and on the breadth of the work to be done. During the interviews, we had spontaneous conversations; then the children told their dreams, which were always tape-recorded, and then drew or painted their dreams. If they did not have any dreams, they made a drawing or painting anyway. Occasionally, and when they asked for it, I read them a story.

All the dream reports were systematically tape-recorded and later transcribed. Due to their phantasmagorical contents, and due to the limitations of the verbal expression of five-year-olds, recordings of dreams could be played over and over, and the meanings intended could be accurately known.

The children also drew or painted their dreams systematically. Their graphic representations of dreams gave precious support to the collecting of dreams. They served as a complement to the verbal account of the dreams by providing information that the child inevitably left out: the proportion of dream figures with regard to one another, their placement in space, their shapes and colors. Sometimes details became precise, and some clarification occurred by drawing or painting the dreams. Usually the graphic representations of the dreams followed the verbal accounts. Occasionally a child would insist on drawing the dream directly and then commented on the drawing.

The materials used for drawing and painting the dreams were white paper (eighteen by twenty-four inches and eighteen by twelve inches), Buffalo sharp-point felt-tipped pens in thirty-six colors, paintbrushes, and watercolor paints. In most instances, children used the large-size paper. They drew their dreams with the felt-tipped pens much more often than they painted them.

In addition to recording the dreams on tape and having children make a graphic representation of their dream, two other procedures were used according to the situation: questioning and unstructured, or free, activities. The interview was oriented toward the discovery of the child's experience and not the verification of a hypothesis. My questions of the children during the interviews were most often aimed at verifying what pertained to the dream experience and what pertained to waking reality. For example: "When you get out of your bed, is it for real or is it in your dream?" I also tried to learn what belonged to the nocturnal dream and what belonged to fantasy: "Is it a dream or a story?"

In other instances, my questions were aimed at obtaining information on the context surrounding a dream event, especially bad dreams. I asked when the dream had occurred—last night or a while ago—whether the child had awakened, what the emotion was upon awakening, and whether the child went to her or his parents. These questions shed light on the nature of each dream and its context. They assisted the collecting of dreams without the use of a systematic list of questions.

The free activities that the children pursued were storytelling, drawing and painting, and the creation of stories. These free activities placed my collecting of dreams within a broader framework of encounter between the children and me. In this way, children could bring dreams when there were dreams, while our encounters followed their course. Without pressuring the children to produce dream reports or putting singular emphasis on dream experience, I could collect dreams without specially rewarding the child-dreamers.

Of the three free activities, drawing and painting were by far the most frequent. I collected forty-five drawings and paintings done by thirteen children.

These were both realistic (house, garden, human figures, the sun) and phantasmagorical (monsters, the sun killing a maniac with its rays). Some were inspired by the child's experience of a fairy tale (Hansel and Gretel, the Three Little Pigs) or of a film like *Star Wars*.

Storytelling was the second most frequent activity. I had seven children's books with stories on the theme of dreams. Listed below are the French titles, and within parentheses their meaning in English or their corresponding English titles.

Bedford, D. de. 1976. *Le joyeux fantôme* [The Joyous Phantom]. Paris: Grasset-Jeunesse.

Brennan, N. 1976. *La veste magique* [The Magic Coat]. Paris: Casterman.

Dumas, P. 1977. *La petite géante* [The Little Giant]. Paris: Ecole des Loisirs.

Francis, F. 1971. *Le papier magique*. Paris: Edition La Farandole [*The Magic Wallpaper*. London: Abelard-Schuman, 1970].

Janosch. 1977. *Une leçon de rêve pour un petit loir* [A Lesson on Dreams for a Little Dormouse]. Paris: Casterman.

Michels, T., and J. Gerber. 1976. *Xandi et le monstre* [Xandi and the Monster]. Paris: Casterman.

Sendak, M. 1963. *Max et les maximonstres*. Haarlem, Holland: Delpire éditeur [*Where the Wild Things Are*. New York: Harper and Row, 1963].

The two stories used for the first interview were *La petite géante* with one group and *Le papier magique* with the three other groups. Stories portraying monsters such as *Max et les maximonstres* and *Xandi et le monstre* were avoided during those first encounters because of the impact they could have had on the children, such as a tendency to associate dreams with dreams of monsters. Later, I read all the stories, and at the request of the children especially *Max et les maximonstres*, *Xandi et le monstre*, *La petite géantre* and *Le papier magique*. The creation of stories was infrequent. Only four girls created stories.

These activities did not lead to a systematic compilation of results, since they were not the object of the study, but part of the context created to collect the dreams.

The key to the interview resides in the relationship that is established between interviewer and child.[5] It is the interviewer who sets the tone of the encounter through her or his presence and the depth of her or his listening. This quality of presence requires preparation and consciousness on the part of the adult. It presupposes that the adult comes empty-handed and creates a psychic space where the child's experience may unfold without inhibition.

For an interview like this, the interviewer and the child step out of linear time, which pushes, presses, and runs, in order to enter into present time, which opens and allows a living contact between participants in the exchange.

The interviewer's awareness of what a privilege it is that children share their psychic experience assures a sensitivity of presence. This sensitivity of presence is necessary because dreams pertain to the child's most intimate inner life, which must be approached with respect for and gratitude to the child.

Chapter Two

What Boys and Girls Dream About

D uring eleven weeks of collecting dreams, I collected 103 reports that the children identified as dreams, 45 drawings and paintings, and 4 stories. With the dream reports, fourteen children reported an average of 7.3 dreams each.[1]

My exploration of the dream material that the children had given me was spirallike and resembled a circumambulation. Circumambulation, or "circular walking," changes the perspective of the one who walks in a spiral. Thus each circling toward the center brought a new focus of interest, and each circling led to discoveries. First, I focused on the content of the dreams and the themes, settings, and challenges they portrayed for both boys and girls. But what struck me from the beginning was how the dreams of children were diverse and alterable.

Children's Dreams: Diverse and Alterable

The reports of what the children identified as dreams showed great diversity. They included nocturnal dreams and what more closely resembled daydreams. They included fragments of dreams and whole dreams that came as scenarios with development, high point, and resolution (consistent with Jung's [1960] description of the average dream). They included fantasies fed by nocturnal fears, and also nocturnal visions and simple fantasies. In addition to diversity, these dreams showed wide variation in esthetic quality, as judged by their dramatic intensity, degree of unity, and power of evocation.

The following examples illustrate the diversity of forms in which the dream reports of the children came:

Marie: Sometimes one may dream of a bottle that moves. Once I dreamed of that. . .it was on the windowsill at my house. And it went "Pts. . .Pts. . .Pts."

Jacques: Last night I dreamed that in my mother's doorway there was a man who walked and who was all white.

Françoise: I had a dream. I thought that I was in the jungle. Then I saw a big mean snake. Then I saw a big water. And the snake was gone into the water. So it did not know where I was anymore. So I walked on my road. I found my road. Then I went to bed in my room.

Later, Françoise commented on her drawing:

I was running. I swam up to here. Then, I took a road, while it found this in the water. . . . It found something to eat instead of me.

Michel: I was in a car. I am coming to hockey. I put my clothes on. Afterward, I shoot the puck and it gets into the goal.

Hélène: One time I dreamed that my parents were robbers. That is true. They had robbed jewelry. They had been put in jail because they had robbed jewelry.

Lucie: Me, in my dream last night, it is that there was a little man that walked in the grass. And he had not seen that there was a magician. And the magician had found the little man. And he had transformed him into a giraffe. And his mother said, "Well, where is my little boy?" And the magician did not know, and he said, "I am sorry, ma'am." And he brought him back into a little guy. And with his house he went back.

Lucie: There was a baby-sitter. And we had all buried her in a big hole. She dug herself up all by herself. After we installed our swimming pool. And she will never, never return again.

Jacques (draws his dream and comments): Clouds hid the sun. Drip, drop, drip, drop. The rain! The sun now was here [under the rainbow]. It heats up clear and clean. There, this is the biggest green mountain. That mountain, it could come up on the clouds. There, there was a square to stand on sometimes, a big one! After that, Robert stood there with his arms up in the air. He was trying to touch the sun. He touched a little. But it was much too hot. He was burning his fingers. Each time that I myself touched the moon, I froze my fingers.

Pierre: I was walking with my friend François. And I hurt him. And he went to tell his father. And after he [François' father] shot the bullet at me. And it had gotten all flat. And it had fallen to the ground. François said, "Hey, are you bionic?" And after, it's the end.

What was an authentic dream? What should be eliminated as invalid data in the framework of the present research on children's dreams, and in the name of which criterion? Louise Bates Ames (1964) observed that children often dream of objects in their rooms. Did Marie's image of the bottle that moves correspond to an improvised fantasy, or to a dream fragment she remembered? Lucie's story of the little man transformed into a giraffe seemed to develop like a confabulation. This motif of magical transformation is nevertheless typical of the child's imaginary thinking. There are similar examples in the data collected by Louis Breger (1969) in his home laboratory study on children's dreams.

What was the nature of the dream of the man who was all white in the bedroom doorway of Jacques's mother? To which type of nocturnal perception did this dream refer? What pertained to the dream, and what pertained to the elaboration of that dream, in Françoise's adventure with the serpent in the jungle? How should the realism in Michel's hockey dream be considered, especially in light of David Foulkes's (1967, 1971; Foulkes et al. 1969) insistence on the realistic character of children's dreams? The contours of the dreams of the parent-robbers and of the buried baby-sitter seem more like the average dream, whereas Pierre's dream of the bullet illustrates one of those sudden reversals of fate characteristic of dreams. Was Jacques's dream of the sun and the moon close to those children's dreams with cosmic themes about which Jung wrote?

In addition to this diversity, the dream reports of children sometimes changed when they drew them. Sometimes the dreams were elaborated and developed for one or more additional interviews. Thus François introduced three policemen into the drawing of his monster dream, who put the monster in a cage and killed it. Jacques reported a monster dream, and a week later he returned to the same theme with the same characters he had now developed, continuing the encounter from the previous week to a resolution. In the initial version of Odile's dream, Geri, a fictional character, was lost in the forest; in the drawing of the dream, it was Odile who was at the center of the action, lost in the forest, and calling for help. Which versions should be retained for analysis? And to which extent could a dream be considered separately from the development it undergoes, secondary versions, and alterations to which it leads?

Since children's dreams are diverse and subject to alteration, they raise in acute terms the question of defining what a dream is. The universe of dreams is a vast and complex reality,[2] a reality that persists as we approach the dreams of children. The literature on the dreams of children offers examples of "big dreams" (Fordham 1969; Jacobi 1971; Wickes 1978), flying dreams (Arnold-Forster 1921), and anticipatory dreams (Barber 1973; Young 1977), as well as references to hypnagogic imaging and half-sleep visions (Ajuriaguerra 1974).

It would, however, be unrealistic to expect young children to distinguish between hypnagogic images seen at the onset of sleep, dreams with which they awake in the morning, night visions or fantasies that nourish their fear of the dark, and extrasensory perceptions that they might have in broad daylight. Children are more likely to call all of these experiences "dreams" without distinction, as long as they involve inner vision.

Furthermore, far from being static, a dream is a living phenomenon subject to processes of alteration.[3] With children the phenomenon of dream alteration takes on special proportions. First, in a young child the boundaries between dream and reality are not completely established, so that both merge, intrude upon, and interpenetrate each other. Jean Piaget (1979) and, following him, Monique Laurendeau and Adrien Pinard (1962) have rigorously described the stages through which the dream conception of children between four and twelve passes. The young child does not yet have a complete notion of dreams. He or she might conceive that the dream originates from an external source, "from the window" perhaps or "from the night," and that it takes place outside the child, for example in the child's bedroom. The child also holds the dream to be "true." From a realistic conception of dreams, the child grows toward a gradually more mature understanding of the internal and immaterial character of dreams (see Appendix for a fuller description of this process).

Finally, the child naturally confabulates, and dreams stimulate the imagination in a very vivid way. "We have all seen," remark Steven Luria Ablon and John E. Mack (1980, 183), "children who, after having reported a dream, develop it in the form of an imaginary narrative." Children live in close rapport with their dreams and spontaneously work on them. They replay them, prolong them and complete them. Children enter their dreams, inhabit them, sometimes substitute themselves for a dream character, or create allies for facing the challenges met in dreams.

The difficulty in researching children's dreams comes, on the one hand, from the nature of dreams. They are many-layered and subject to alteration. On the other hand, the difficulty comes from the mental functioning of children, for whom dreams are closely continuous with fantasies, the one easily influencing the other. Research on children's dreams must be able to rely on an open and nuanced conception of dreams in order to include the many kinds of dreams that the child might encounter and the modifications and transformations that these dreams might undergo due to the child's active imagination, insofar as these modifications are in line with the development of the dreams and come, like the dreams, from the child's unconscious.

After considering these factors, I chose to retain all that children themselves had identified as dreams, although I was aware that these reports of dreams included dreams of different kinds accessed at different moments in their evolution. From the point of view of the following study of the contents of dreams, the question of the distinction between different kinds of dreams and different times in their evolution recedes in favor of the themes present in the dreams, the settings in which they take place, and the attitudes that the children adopt in confronting the challenges in their dreams.

The Contents of the Dreams

In the dreams of children a whole universe unfolded, including night and shadow, day and light, and the elements of water, earth, fire, and air. Water engulfed and drowned, dragged into currents, and also protected; it was the water of the river, the ocean, the swimming pool, the stream, the waterfall, the lake, and the rain. Earth came in the form of the forest and the jungle, where the children got lost, where they met the wolf, the serpent, the crocodile, and the elves; the earth appeared as a high and pointed mountain or a rounded mountain with a cavern dug into it, as the lair of the monster and the summit of the world, as the garden, the burial place, the hole, and as the hydra flower. The thunderbolt, the conflagration, and the dragon's breath were all made of fire. The element of air appeared as stars, space, clouds, a storm; with birds, a flying man, a flying house, and a flying saucer.

In this universe there were also the animals—crocodiles, serpents, elephants, wolves, sharks, whales, lions, dogs, birds, bees, and caterpillars—which bit, chased, stung, and devoured, and which the children attacked, fled, thwarted, or tamed.

And then in this universe there were the monsters, some half animal and half human, ghostly, fabulous, or terrible. There were the objects, both familiar and numinous,[4] such as a mirror, jewelry, sandals, a powder machine, houses both magnificent and burnt. And there were humans: parents, father, mother, grandparents, brothers, sisters, friends, neighbors, robbers, gangsters, the bus driver, the baby sitter, the unknown stranger, the child, the savior, the companion—and the characters taken from television, movies, or childhood literature, such as the Bionic woman, King Kong, Luke Skywalker, Cinderella, and Little Red Riding Hood.

The dream settings went from the familiar surroundings of the child's bedroom, parents' bedroom, living room, and other rooms, toward the outside of the house, the porch, the backyard, the sidewalk, the garage, the immediate neighborhood, the street, the larger neighborhood, to other houses such as that of the grandparents, the cottage, the houses of friends, and to public places such as the store, the park, the prison, the restaurant, the reception hall, the movie theater, and to buses, boats, train tracks, a foreign city, and into nature—to the sea, the mountain, the forest, the grass, and the garden.

Certain dreams were humorous, others numinous. In a large proportion of the dreams, there was a challenge that the dreams sent the dreamers. Monsters appeared in the children's bedrooms or along their paths, animals chased them, objects moved and changed shape. In their dreams, the children were the victims of aggression or of train and car accidents (see fig. 1). The children fell into emptiness or into water. They got lost, they lost an object, or were robbed. They were threatened by the forces of nature, as in the collapse of the earth, fires, and so forth. They died or were eaten by the monster.

Faced with the challenges they encountered in their dreams, the children had different responses. In some cases, the way out was to wake up and find refuge with an adult who was in the house. But in the dreams themselves, children sometimes described themselves as visual witnesses to the situation without their active engagement in it. In other dreams, the children reacted by crying and went to adults to be consoled, or the children screamed and cried out for help, or escaped and sometimes thereby misled their enemies. Sometimes children were saved by means of good fortune, as for example when a small floating seat was in the water of the river into which a child had fallen. Or the children were saved by the intervention of an ally, most often an adult (police officer, stranger, parent), who came to the child's rescue at a timely moment and solved the problem of the dream. Finally, sometimes the children plunged into the action themselves. Sometimes this took the form of coping with the misdeeds of the monster after the fact, or actively confronting the danger directly, but with the help of an ally—a parent, a friend, an imaginary companion endowed with magical powers—or with the help of a natural force such as water or fire. In other dreams, children faced the danger alone, without help, and adopted an attitude toward the threatening character that was active, experimental, direct, and confrontive or affirming.

There were also dreams that did not involve any direct response on the part of the dreamers or their allies. The dream ended on a fact: the child had fallen, had been hit by a train, burnt in a fire, robbed, or had died in an accident.

Gender Differences: Themes, Settings, Responses to Challenges

Of the 103 dreams identifed as such by the children, 59 were reported by girls and 44 by boys. The boys produced 27 drawings, and the girls 18. The four stories were created by girls.

I identified eight main themes. For the dreams taken as a whole, human characters appeared in 79.6 percent, monsters in 25.2 percent, animals in 25.2 percent, and characters from television, children's books, and movies in 10.6 percent of the dreams. The themes of earth, water, air, and fire were present at 19.4 percent for earth, 16.5 percent for water, 12.6 percent for air, and 11.6 percent for fire.

Figure 1. Painting 24" x 18" (for all the paintings and drawings, the first measurement refers to the length and the second to the width). The car accident. While their father is inside the store, Mireille and her sister play with the steering. The car rolls down the hill and catches fire. On the hill, the store is on the right, the rolling car is in the center, and at the bottom is the car on fire. The sun is above.

Proportions of these main themes for boys and girls pointed to gender differences (see Table 1). The theme of the monster was clearly more prominent for boys. It was six times more frequent for boys than for girls. The category "monster" includes phantasmagorical beings, fabulous animals, human types of monsters, and a hydra flower. The monsters in boys' dreams were generally phantasmagorical and often huge: a gigantic dragon, a vampire-insect, a spider that makes one sick, an apocalyptic monster, a half-human half-animal beast with pincers for hands, a head with a floating and ghostly body, a head with vibrating contours affixed to a robust square body, a flying man, a dark character, and so on.

As well as being less frequent, the monsters in girls' dreams were smaller and more realistic: a dark head with flaming red eyes seen in a tree in the woods, a green man with a pocket in his belly for children, a salesman who is a monster, a hydra flower.

Table 1

Proportion of eight themes in the dreams of boys, girls, and both together[a]

Theme	Boys	Girls	Both
Monster	47.7%	8.4%	25.2%
Animal	11.3	35.5	25.2
Characters (TV, books, movies)	11.3	10.1	10.6
Humans	90.0	71.1	79.6
mother	15.9	10.1	12.6
father/grandfather	11.3	15.2	13.5
Water	27.7	8.4	16.5
Earth	9.0	27.1	19.4
Air	18.1	8.4	12.6
Fire	11.3	11.8	11.6

[a] The total of proportions for the eight themes under "Both" is equal to or more than one hundred because one dream sometimes contained more than one theme.

The animal theme, by contrast, was three times more frequent for girls. For all the boys and for most of the girls, dream animals duplicated the functions of monsters in that they had a threatening character and exerted an engrossing effect on the child's attention. The dream animals included serpents, crocodiles, wolves, elephants, and others, and they chased, bit, and otherwise threatened the children. Other animals, only in girls' dreams, illustrated the phenomena of birth, reproduction, and family life (the birth of baby cats, a family of worms). In girls' dreams there was also the motif of the bird that was caught, which occurred in two dreams.

Characters taken from television, children's books, and movies were present in the dreams of girls and boys almost equally. Human characters such as father, mother, and friends appeared in most boys' dreams (90 percent). For girls, references to humans were less numerous. Mother figures appeared in boys' dreams more than father figures and grandfather figures taken together. For girls, this ratio was reversed, and a father figure was most often portrayed.

The theme of water clearly predominated in boys' dreams. Boys fell into water five times in boys' dreams. Water was also often linked to the monster in boys' dreams: from the water the monster emerged, through contact with water the monster disappeared, the monster climbed into a boat in the water, water engulfed what the monster had destroyed, the water from the waterfall came into the cavern of the monster. The theme of water was less frequent for girls. Girls did not fall into water, as boys did. A girl drowned, however. Monsters and water were also linked in girls' dreams: water inhibited the serpent's pursuit of the dreamer, a sea monster lived in the water.

For girls, the theme of the earth was as frequent as the theme of water for boys. Girls got lost in the forest. In the forest they met the serpent, the wolf, the monster. The forest was thus a place of adventure. Other symbols of the earth theme in girls' dreams were the mountain, the garden, the person or object buried. Earth symbols were less frequent in boys' dreams, but they were of the same kind: the forest and the mountain were also places of encounter with the monster, the mountain was the summit of the world. For boys there was also the motif of the destruction of the earth.

The theme of air was two times more frequent for boys than for girls. The theme of fire was as frequent for boys as for girls. The motif of the house that burns down was the most frequent. That house was sometimes the house of the dreamer, sometimes the house of friends; sometimes the owner was not specified. Like water, fire was linked to the monster. For boys, there was a dragon that spat fire, a monster that caused the house to be on fire, the fire that destroys the enemy monsters, the electricity that metamorphoses the monster; for girls, there was the monster with the flaming eyes.

For analyzing the settings of the dreams, each dream was classified only once, following the explicit identification of the settings from the girl or the boy dreamers themselves, either from a verbal account of the dream or from the drawing or painting of the dream. When dreams referred to more than one setting, the setting in which the central event of the dream took place or the setting in which the dream culminated was selected. In all other cases, when the dreams described characters or events without explicit reference to any setting, even if the setting could have been inferred, the dreams were considered to have occurred in an imprecise setting.

Dreams took place in the house, in the environs of the house (patio, backyard, street), and in other familiar settings (grandparents' house, friend's house, vacation house) in the following proportions: 28.1 percent in the house, 6.7 percent in the environs of the house, and 2.9 percent in other familiar settings. Dreams took place in public settings (store, jail), in outdoor settings (foreign city, train track), and in nature (ocean, mountain), in the following proportions: 7.7 percent in public settings, 5.8 percent in outdoor settings, and 24.2 in nature. In 24.2 percent of the dreams, the setting remained imprecise.

The proportions among different types of settings for boys' and girls' dreams showed gender differences (see Table 2). In boys' dreams, the highest incidence of dreams occurred in the house (38.6 percent), generally in the dreamer's house and occasionally in the house of another central character in the dream, and thus the setting was indoors and in a well-known place. In girls' dreams, by contrast, the highest incidence of dreams occurred in nature (28.8 percent), and thus outdoors. The proportion of dreams in which the setting remained imprecise was comparable for boys and girls. The other types of settings showed no appreciable differences. Dreams occuring in public settings were as frequent for boys as for girls. There was a slightly higher incidence of dreams set in the environs of the house and in other familiar settings for girls, and a slightly higher incidence of dreams in outdoor settings such as foreign cities and train tracks for boys.

The proportion of dreams describing threatening situations or raising challenges for the children, such as those portraying monsters, threatening animals, bizarre objects, or such events as accidents, being robbed, or coming to grips with a natural force, was clearly higher for boys than for girls. In fact, 77.2 percent of dreams reported by boys had these qualities, whereas only 47.4 percent of those told by girls had them (see Table 3).

Boys and girls differed in the proportion of types of response to challenges (see Table 4). With regard to challenging situations encountered in their dreams, boys more often than girls took an active stance, whether or not they received some kind of assistance. More often than girls, boys were saved by the advent of a fortunate occurrence, or by the magical action of a natural force. For girls, the challenge dreams resulted more often in some kind of "symbolic death" in the form of being robbed, getting lost, knocked down, or devoured. Girls called for help more often, whereas boys had to flee more often. Boys and girls were rescued by someone else's intervention in nearly the same measure. And boys reacted by crying almost as often as girls.

Analyzing gender differences permits the identification of gender-influenced themes, settings, and responses. But what is the meaning of the high proportion of girls' dreams set in nature, and those of boys set in the home? What is the meaning of the high proportion in girls' dreams of the themes of the animal and the earth, and in boys' dreams the monster and water? And what is the meaning of the presence of the father and grandfather figures in girls' dreams and the presence of the mother in boys' dreams? Do these proportions along lines of gender, as well as the high incidence of symbolic death in girls' dreams and the high incidence of active types of response in boys' dreams, hold true for a larger population of children of the same age?

Analysis of the data opened up several avenues of research on these questions. To follow these avenues, it would have been necessary to collect data from many more children from more diverse backgrounds; meanwhile the potential in the data already collected would not have been uncovered. At the heart of the data was the monster, which required more exploration.

Table 2

Proportion of seven types of settings in the
dreams of boys, girls, and both together

Type of Setting	Boys	Girls	Both
In the house (child's room, parents' room, living room, play room, from one room to the next and nearby)	38.6%	20.3%	28.1%
In the environs of the house (balcony, backyard, garage, neighborhood, street, school, connected dwelling units)	4.5	8.4	6.7
Other familiar settings (grandparents' house, friend's, vacation house)	0	5.0	2.9
Public settings (store, park, prison, restaurant, movie theater, bus, hockey field)	6.8	8.4	7.7
Other outdoor settings (foreign city, railroad tracks, roof, swimming pool, hill)	9.0	5.0	5.8
In nature (water, boat, mountain, forest, jungle, grass, garden, tree, air)	15.9	28.8	24.2
Imprecise settings	24.9	23.7	24.2

Table 3

Proportion of challenge dreams of
boys, girls, and both together

Boys	Girls	Both
77.2%	47.4%	61.1%

Table 4

Proportion of twelve types of response to challenges
in the dreams of boys, girls, and both together

Type of Response to Challenge	Boys	Girls	Both
Adopt active attitude without assistance	23.5%	7.1%	16.1%
Adopt active attitude with assistance (ally or magical aid)	20.5	3.5	12.9
Contend with monster's misdeeds and damage	2.9	3.5	3.2
Be saved or consoled by someone	14.7	17.5	16.1
Be saved by good fortune or magical action of an element	14.7	3.5	6.4
Flee	11.7	7.1	9.6
Call for help	0	10.7	4.8
Cry	2.9	3.5	1.6
Be witness to, watch	2.9	7.1	4.8
Wake oneself up	2.9	10.7	6.4
Fall, be thrown into water, be eaten, be burned, be smashed into, die	8.8	28.5	17.7
None	17.6	21.4	19.0

[a] The total of proportions for the twelve types of response under "Both" is equal to or more than one hundred because one dream sometimes contained more than one response.

Chapter Three

Strategies for Encountering the Monster

The monster mobilized the psychic energy of the child. So far the category "monster" has referred to monsters of a phantasmagorical nature, including monsters in human form. But as we have seen, such dream animals as the serpent, the crocodile, the wolf, and the elephant functioned in children's dreams as monsters in that they threatened the child and had an engrossing effect on the child's attention. If I added together all the dreams centering on the theme of the monster, and on animals that functioned like monsters, then over a third of the dreams reported by the children in this study, some forty-five in all, portrayed an encounter between a child and a monster. The strategies for encountering the monster, in phantasmagorical, animal, or human form, became my focus.

The questions of why the theme of the monster was so prominent in children's dreams, what this theme meant as a psychological dynamic, and what the monster represented were deferred until a long incursion into the heart of the data provided a basis for understanding (see Chapter 8). At this stage it proved more opportune to center on the ways children encountered the monster and coped with it.

The monster took on its full meaning through relationship with the dreamer. It is the dynamic between child and monster that required investigation. The monster called the child forth and the child called the monster forth. The monster challenged the child and by so doing required that the child mobilize and respond: escape, attack, combat, death of the monster, or else approach, exploration, and transformation of the monster or symbolic death through the monster.

I began to look at the activity of the child who was relating to the monster. What was the goal of the child's activity? Did this activity aim at controlling, exterminating, foiling, or taming the monster? And what actions did the child use in the interaction? For example, how was the monster exterminated? Was it knocked down with a stick or forced backward into a chimney and burned? Did the child face the monster alone or with the help of an ally? Was that ally an adult or a peer, a female or a male? Was this encounter with the monster undergone with magical help—for example, the help of some force of nature such as fire or water—or with the help of a dream character endowed with magical powers? Did that child or the child's ally use a weapon? Which weapon?

All these components in the encounter with the monster, including the goal and kind of activity, recourse to an ally or not, the presence or absence of magical help, and the use or nonuse of a weapon, defined aspects of the *strategy*, or "plan of action," with which dreamers coped with the monsters in their dreams.

Goal and Nature of the Actions Used

Identifying a strategy's goal required from me a certain level of interpretation of the activities of the dreamers. The goal of their actions could only be identified afterward and from the end result reached by the strategy. I tried to remain as close as possible to the facts of the dreams, and to preserve the diversity that characterized the strategies I observed. The goal and the nature of the activities are here presented parallel and together.

The strategies that I observed aimed at an emotional release through crying, at finding refuge and consolation by being next to an adult, at calling for help, at fleeing the monster, at foiling it, at using guile such as substituting another in one's place, at controlling the monster by putting it in a cage, at stopping it or containing it in a restricted space, at attacking it from a distance with a weapon such as a stone or stick, at coping with the monster's misdeeds and the damage it caused by tending one's wound or extinguishing a fire the monster started, at exterminating the monster by knocking, combating, pushing into a fire, eating, or killing it. Other strategies aimed at approaching the monster to observe it in its lair or touch it, at making it emerge by means of a magical transformation using objects or water or electricity, at taming the monster by stroking it, at getting it to disappear by touching it, at annulling its malefic power by adopting a certain attitude, or at entering into the belly of the monster and being engulfed.

Allies, Magical Help, Weapons

The strategies used in dreams to cope with the phenomenon of the monster often included the intervention of another character who brought some kind of assistance to the child. Those characters who contributed to the resolution of the problem of the monster were defined as allies. The dreams showed two main types of allies, those who were adults and those who were the child's peers. There were also circumstances in which the encounter between the child and the monster excluded the presence and the intervention of any other character. It then took the form of an intimate and direct contact between the child and the monster whereby the child had recourse to his or her own resources, as observed, for instance, in the taming of the monster.

Sometimes the child received magical help, assisted by a dream character, object, or natural element, which was invested with powers that went beyond its ordinary nature. For example, the monster died because it came into contact with water. Finally, the child and the ally sometimes used a weapon. The type of weapon used is significant for an understanding of the essential nature of the strategy, since weapons are expressions of the hero, as well as the enemy that the hero fights (Oriol-Boyer 1975).

Gender Differences

The dreams portraying phantasmagorical, animal, or human monsters were, as might be expected, more frequent with boys than with girls: twenty-seven of these dreams came from boys and eighteen from girls. The boys' experience showed a great coherence. It was organized along a continuum that went from recourse to an adult ally, recourse to a peer ally, absence of any ally, and toward a growing capacity on the child's part for taking charge and being responsible for the resolution of the problem raised by the monster.

At one end of the continuum, the child conceived a strategy in which the problem was resolved by means of intervention by an adult ally who substituted for the child in taking action. The adult acted on behalf of the child. Thus, it was the father who stopped the flying man from continuing to break windows and threatening to enter Jean-Louis's bedroom (see fig. 2). And in the drawing of his dream, François had three policemen intervene by putting the monster in a cage and killing it.

In the middle of the continuum, the ally appeared in the two forms of adult and peer in the same dream. Michel was running to his friend for help, but it was his father who came to kill the dragon who spat fire; and in another dream, Michel induced the baby-monster (peer ally) to change into a "papa-monster" (adult ally) who then killed the mama-monster.

Figure 2. Painting 24" x 18". Jean-Louis's father stops the flying man. In front of the house is the father. In the air is the flying man.

Further along, the peer ally assumes predominance. In Eric's dreams, this ally took the form of an imaginary companion endowed with magical powers. Sometimes the imaginary companion took charge of resolving the problem for the child, and sometimes he substituted for the child in the victim role or joined his strength to that of the child. In Jacques's dreams, the peer ally was in the role of the one who accompanied Jacques in all his exploits (see fig. 3).

Finally, at the other end of the continuum, Pierre acted on his own. His mother, who was his ally in one dream, aided in the control of the monster, but it was Pierre who indicated to her how to proceed.

The boys' dreams displayed some twenty-five strategies, and these strategies ranged in their goals among all those goals previously mentioned except for annulling the monster's malefic power and being engulfed. On a few occasions, boys' strategies included recourse to magic. Eric's imaginary companion had the power to disappear when someone such as the enemy monsters touched him, and he immediately reappeared next to the child. For Eric, the magical effect of a triangle lighted a fire in the chimney and burned the

Figure 3. Drawing 24" x 18". Dream represented in a cartoon bubble pointing to the dreamer lying on his two-tier bunk bed. Jacques and his companion walk in the mountains at night. They see two monsters: one sits by the cavern door, the other stands on the top of the cavern.

monsters. Through contact with water, the monster in Pierre's dream disappeared.

A weapon was present in three dreams. An adult ally used a gun in Michel's dream. Jacques knocked the monster down with a stick. Eric used a stone that he threw at a crocodile.

The girls' experience was concentrated in a much smaller number of dreams. But the continuum from adult ally, peer ally, and then recourse to one's own resources was again present. For girls as for boys, the adult ally was generally male (father, grandfather, Tarzan). In Marie's dream, it was the grandfather who killed "the monster with flaming eyes." In Françoise's dream, it was Tarzan who intervened and killed the wolf. But the adult ally also appeared in new roles. Marie's father took Marie in his arms and escaped with her. In another dream, he intervened and gave her what amounts to a lesson: he told her that she had to learn "to play outside even if there were crocodiles and even if they bite" (see fig. 4). Marie's mother, on the other hand, intervened to console Marie when she was in tears. The peer ally appeared in Odile's dream in the form of a paper mannequin, which doubled for the child and thereby tricked the wolf. Marjorie encountered the monster all by herself.

Girls' dreams illustrated fourteen strategies. These dreams did not contain scenes of fighting, as the boys' dreams did. The girls used trickery against the monster and guile (see fig. 5). There was one scene of engulfment. Another strategy for coping with the effects of the monster's misdeeds was for one girl to care for a wound that the monster inflicted. Girls dreams showed no recourse to magic, and no explicit recourse to weapons.

Analyzing the strategies for encountering the monster had brought to light three kinds of recourse: to an adult ally, to a peer ally, to one's own resources. And these kinds of recourse are on a continuum from complete reliance on others to a growing autonomy of the dreamer. Could these three kinds of recourse belong to one unidirectional, sequential model, or could they be better understood as occurring within a cyclical pattern like points along an evolutionary spiral recurring at different intervals?

Analyzing these strategies had also brought out substantial differences between boys and girls in the various configurations of strategy between child and monster. Although one might wonder if the gender differences observed would be verified by data from a large population, it is the meaning of identified gender differences, beyond the question of statistical verification, that called for a deeper elucidation and understanding.

Finally, three major patterns had emerged in the encounter with the monster: combat, taming, and engulfment. For combat, whether the child used trickery with the monster, attempted to control it or exterminate it, the child was involved in a pattern of encountering the monster by combat. By exploring and approaching the monster, various forms of moving toward the monster that culminated in taming were enacted. Engulfment expressed a distinctive rapport between the child and the monster. The meaning of combat, taming, and engulfment in the intimacy of the transaction between child and monster led me to an ever-deeper inquiry.

Centering on Three Strategies: Combat, Taming, and Engulfment

Centering on three strategies led to selecting and amplifying three dream series. The way to amplify a dream series—that is, elucidate its meaning—is presented in Chapter 4.

Strategies could only be described fully in the context of the dreams in which they were employed and the dream series in which they were embedded. They were intelligible only in their relationship to the monsters that had evoked

Figure 4. Drawing 18" x 12". In front of Marie's house there are crocodiles that bite her. On the left side of the narrow patio is a crocodile. In the center is the house. On the right stands Marie. Above are the clouds and sun.

Figure 5. Drawing 24" x 18". From left to right: the sun, a tree, the lake where the snake finds something to eat in place of Françoise, Françoise, the snake chasing her, Françoise back in her house.

them. The monster and its actions had to be described. Discerning the moment in which, and the place where, the encounter between monster and girl or boy dreamer had occurred, whether it was during the day or at night, out in nature or in the child's bedroom, what role natural elements played, as well as other significant symbols—all became crucial to this enterprise.

Each child had reported between one and nine dreams on the theme of the monster. Taken in their chronological order, these dreams of each child constituted a series of dreams on the theme studied. Some of these series illustrated a process that evolved toward a resolution of the problem the monster posed in the first dreams of each series. In these cases, in order to bring out the dynamic dimension of the dreams, it was necessary to describe the strategies from the perspective of their evolution through all the dreams constituting a series.

Two series included a large number of dreams centering on the theme of the encounter with the monster. The first series, Eric's, included eight dreams, all of which focused on the phenomenon of combating the monster. The second series, Pierre's, contained eight dreams, out of eleven, that focused on the monster with the child. In spite of the exclusion of three dreams from Pierre's series, the remaining dreams were sufficiently rich to treat this series, like the first, through a dynamic perspective. Pierre's series illustrated the phenomenon of taming the monster.

The other series, the majority, included one to four dreams on the monster theme. In these short series, when the dreams succeeded one another, the dynamic link uniting them could sometimes be grasped; but when the dreams spread out through time, and intervening dreams centering on nonmonster themes were missing, the dreams of these short series fell like isolated points along a curve, and the dynamics of the dream process became imperceptible. It was thus necessary to work with integral series of dreams that were long enough for the dynamic dimension to show clearly.

Eric's series conformed to these criteria. As for Pierre's series, it required only that the three nonmonster dreams be included in the series for the series to be complete. Among all the remaining series, Marjorie's was distinctive: it included, altogether, eleven dreams, four of which portrayed child and monster together, in relationship, and it illustrated the phenomenon of engulf-ment by the monster.

The three series selected met the criteria for length and thematic unity, but they were also characterized by their authenticity. That is, they showed no trace of external influences. I have already explained that the first interview took place in a group, and I had noted four instances of children influencing one another's dream reports. Eric and Pierre were the ones whose dream reports had given rise to imitation by others, perhaps because of the power of their experience. But the opposite had not happened—Eric and Pierre were not influenced by the dream reports of others. And Marjorie's experience was unique.

Some of the series collected included strong dreams, but they were dreamed before the study. However rich these dreams were, they did not have the potential for engaging the dreamer in a present-time dynamic process of the psyche. The dreams of the three series selected were by all appearance the expression of a process lived in the present and tapped into live at the moment when the dreams were collected.

Each of the three series constituted a whole, insofar as the problem of the monster stated at the beginning developed toward some form of resolution. In this sense, a certain coherence arose from these series. Finally, a vitality and a particular force characterized these series. Many of their dreams contained symbols that were rich and full of meaning.

The other complete series had one of these disqualifying limitations: either they contained too few dreams, only three to five; or the texture of certain dreams lacked in force or consistency; or the dreams, powerful as they were, referred to the past.

By themselves, the three series contained thirty dreams, almost a third of all the dreams collected. All the major themes present in the dreams collected were found in these three series: water, fire, earth, air, monsters, animals, objects, different settings such as a child's bedroom and house, local neighborhood, foreign city, nature, and a good number of challenges from fire, the collapse of the earth, accidents, falls, a chase. Two series came from the dream experience of boys, and a third described the dream experience of a girl. The series contained nocturnal dreams, and also, by their appearance, dreams developed by the child's imaginative power.

These three series, then, reflected the whole collection from which they were drawn, both in the themes covered and in how gender correlated to these themes.

Chapter Four

Amplifying Children's Dream Series

Amplifying a series of dreams from a child makes it possible to observe a larger dream process at work than a study of isolated dreams would permit. Deeper meanings and a better grasp of the unfolding movement of the dreams emerge from observing dreams in this way. My practice of dream amplification is inspired by Carl Jung's way of working with dreams.

The Dynamic Dimension of Dreams

At first glance, the dreams reported by the same dreamer might seem disparate and unconnected to one another. By itself, each dream is already an enigma. When the number of dreams increases, resolving the enigma would seem to become more complex. Actually it is simplified. Of course, the data have increased in size and number of details, but it becomes easier to grasp the general movement of the whole and to formulate a hypothesis about the direction of the series, a hypothesis that will later be verified or not through individual analysis of the dreams in the series.

Jung (1954) noted that working with series of dreams increases the reliability of their interpretation, for if errors slip in during the course of the process of interpretation, these can be corrected by later dreams. "Every interpretation is an hypothesis, an attempt to read an unknown text. An obscure dream, taken in isolation, can hardly ever be interpreted with any certainty. For this reason I attach little importance to the interpretation of single dreams. A relative degree of certainty is reached only in the interpretation of a series of dreams, where the later dreams correct the mistakes we have made in handling those that went before. Also, the basic ideas and themes can be recognized much better in a dream-series. And I therefore urge my patients to keep a careful record of their dreams and of the interpretations given" (150). Oneiric life has its own movement. Far from being isolated fragments, dissociated from one another, dreams hang together, amplify one another, and gather in constellations. This is not by accident but according to an order, a logic that has direction and meaning for the psychic life of the dreamer.

Jung (1953a) suggested that in spite of their great diversity and apparent incoherence, dreams as manifestations of unconscious processes are organized around an integrating principle, around a center or a centered disposition, and follow a course that resembles a spiral moving toward its center:

> The way is not straight but appears to go round in circles. More accurate knowledge has proved it to go in spirals. The dream-motifs always return after certain intervals to definite forms, whose characteristic it is to define a centre. And as a matter of fact the whole process revolves about a central point or some arrangement around a centre, which may in certain circumstances appear even in the initial dreams. As manifestations of unconscious processes the dreams rotate or circumambulate round the centre, drawing closer to it as the amplification increases in distinctness and in scope. Owing to the diversity of the symbolical material it is difficult at first to perceive any kind of order at all. Nor should it be taken for granted that dream sequences are subject to any governing principle. But, as I say, the process of development proves on closer inspection to be cyclic or spiral. (28)

Indeed, the movement of dreams is not foreign to the conscious life of their dreamers. There is a continuous dynamic interaction between the conscious and the unconscious life out of which the movement of psychic experience emerges. Dreams and symbols freely release energies that influence the dreamer's conscious life. Once integrated into the conscious life of the dreamer, symbolic contents thus modified again act on the field of unconscious forces and modify them. "Symbols have at once an *expressive* and *impressive* character," observes Jacobi; "on the one hand they express the intrapsychic process in images; but, on the other hand, when they have become image, 'incarnated' as it were in a pictorial material, they 'make an impression,' that is, their meaning content influences the intrapsychic process and furthers the flow of psychic energy" (Jacobi 1973, 94).

The purpose of the present work with dream series is not to study the dynamic interaction existing between children's dreams and their lives as it would be in a clinical setting. It is to tracking the perceptible movement from one dream to the next through a dream series. The thread of this dynamic analysis is organized around the dreamer as portrayed within his or her dreams. It consists in following the dreamer's way through the different dream situations of the series. The focus of the study is on strategies for encountering the monster, and these dreamers' strategies require that the symbolic dimensions of their dreams also be considered.

The Jungian Method of Amplification

The many symbolic elements of a dream series are related to one another at many angles and at many levels. Amplifying the dreams, which is the work of finding the links among these angles and levels, brings these links to light.

My practice of dream amplification follows a method developed by Jung (1953a) that Jung himself borrowed from philology, and it consists in a search for parallel contexts where one finds the same symbol, in order to explore the many possibilities of interpretation of this symbol. A philologist contending with what a rare word means attempts to grasp that meaning by studying the other texts in which the word appears and gradually formulates a hypothesis later to be verified in the initial context from which the word comes. In the same way, the analyst or researcher of dreams gets to the meaning of a symbolic motif by looking for parallel contexts where that same motif is found—in myths, fairy tales, legends, historical symbolism, the psychology of people in other cultures, or any other source likely to bring to clarity the symbolic motif studied. "In Jung's amplification method," observes Jolande Jacobi, "the various dream motifs are enriched by analogous, related images, symbols, legends, myths, etc., which throw light on their diverse aspects and possible meanings, until their significance stands out in full clarity. Each element of meaning thus obtained is linked with the next, until the whole chain of dream motifs is revealed and the whole dream as a unit can be subjected to a final verification" (1973, 86).

Jacobi (1973, 87) illustrates the process of amplification by means of a multidimensional structure (see fig. 6). Starting with four centers—A, B, C, and D—each corresponding to an element of the dream, points around each center connect with each center by rays, and these sets of points describe the circumferences of four circles. From the points at the circumferences, other rays radiate, ending in a second series of circumferences. The concentric and starlike structure thus formed illustrates the amplification of each dream element taken separately. These structures are in their turn linked among themselves, leading to additional structural developments that take domelike shapes. These shapes both extend and contain the preceding geometric elaboration. The structure that results is similar to the complex and subtle structure of a crystal.

Each dream element opens up and unfolds, and each level of opening creates new possibilities of relationship with the other elements. The nature of symbols is such that there is no inherent limit to amplification. Within the con-

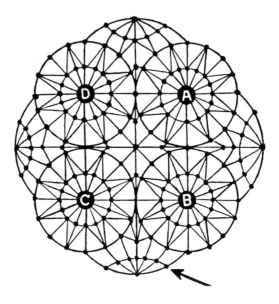

Figure 6. A, B, C, D. The dream elements. The nodal points of the net of connections indicated by the small arrow represent the individual parallels or amplifications.

text of a dream or a series of dreams, however, it is the search for the "nuclear identity" of the whole that regulates the practice of amplification. And this applied amplification reaches its end when the "nuclear meaning" either of the dream or of the dream series seems to have been recognized.

Steps in Amplifying the Dreams

The work of amplification that is presented in the next chapters is the fruit of cooperation between intuition and theoretical research. The first step of this work consists in letting oneself be impregnated by the dreams. Some focal points in the energy of these dreams emerge, and dream motifs call to and echo one another. Symbols first perceived as closed objects open up little by little, releasing their meaning and their liveliness. The dreams unfold. They begin to connect with one another. Hypotheses about the meaning of a symbolic motif, a dream, or the direction of a series form. "It is best to treat a dream as one would a totally unknown object," says Jung. "One looks at it from all sides, one takes it in one's hand, carries it about, has all sorts of ideas and fantasies about it, and talks of it to other people" (1953b, 56).

Amplifying dreams, then, is stimulated by theoretical research on the symbols found in dreams. Starting around 1915, many researchers, including Carl Jung, Mircea Eliade, and then Joseph Campbell and Erich Neumann, have helped make possible the ongoing work of restoring the contact and finding the vitality in the vast symbolic heritage of the past, from which modern humanity, with its rationalistic consciousness, had been cut off. This heritage has been fertilizing modern awareness and connecting it with more remote historico-religious roots. And this heritage offers rich and verdant material for inquiry into symbolic meanings.

This same corrective movement has given rise to a whole array of reference works on symbols and myths, such as dictionaries of symbols and of mythologies (Cirlot 1962; Chevalier and Gheerbrant 1973; de Vries 1974; Hamilton 1942; Grant and Hazel 1981). These works have nothing in common with those codes of fixed and univocal meanings with which dictionaries of symbols have been generally associated. They are like encyclopedias insofar as they gather and juxtapose a great diversity of points of view on a given symbol, multiplying and opening avenues of exploration and research instead of closing them, leaving room for the paradoxical, multidimensional, and changeable nature of symbols. The use of such tools stimulates the work of the imagination. It permits the rapid glance, and simultaneously it permits many possibilities and hypotheses for interpretation, which can be verified later and fed from deeper and more specific research.[1]

The multiplication of points of view to which amplification leads is constantly directed by the search for the meaning of the whole. The many pieces of information gathered on the meaning of a symbol, the associations to which a symbol gives rise, the images and the analogies that could be juxtaposed with it all must be filtered by the dream itself and the dream series in which the dream occurs. Marie-Louise von Franz observed that far from being the result of an arbitrary mental process, amplification is the fruit of a "disciplined imagination": "The method of necessary statement or amplification requires great specific precision. We do not proceed arbitrarily. The associations to a specific symbolic image or a mythological motif use a disciplined imagination. . . . Hence [its] connection with logic and mathematical reasoning."[2]

In the following presentation, the amplification has been as rigorous as possible. On the whole it has stayed close to the original texts of the dreams, with the objective, first, of describing the dreamer's actions, and then elucidating the meaning of the dream without losing touch with the natural flow of the dream and the evolving movement of the series.

The Nature of Symbols

Symbols are the key that unlocks the meaning of the actions that the dreamers perform. Dreams abound in symbols, which are moving in their richness and vitality. Symbols refer to realities that can be sensed. For Jacobi (1973), they are as real as a waterfall is real: "The psychic images in dreams, fantasies, etc. are products and expressions of physical energy, just as a waterfall is a product and an expression of physical energy. For without energy (though the physical concept is only a working hypothesis) there would be no waterfall; and without such concrete manifestations as the waterfall the energy could not be observed and verified. This may sound paradoxical; but paradox is the very essence of all psychic life" (94).

It is this identity between energy and image or, according to Chevalier and Gheerbrant (1973), between "the signified and the signifying," that distinguishes a symbol from a sign: "The symbol differs essentially from the sign insofar as the latter is an arbitrary convention which leaves the sign unconnected to the signifying (object or subject), whereas the symbol presupposes *homogeneity of the signifying and the signified, in the sense that both are an organized dynamism*" (xvii; translated by the author).

Another feature of the symbol is that it expresses a relatively unknown reality that could not otherwise or more fully be expressed in any other way. The sign, on the contrary, always designates something known.

> Every view which interprets the symbolic expression as an analogue or an abbreviated designation for a known thing is *semiotic*. A view which interprets the symbolic expression as the best possible formulation of a relatively unknown thing which cannot for that reason be more clearly or characteristically represented is *symbolic*. A view which interprets the symbolic expression as an intentional paraphrase or transmogrification of a known thing is *allegoric*. An expression that stands for a known thing always remains a mere sign and is never a symbol. It is, therefore, quite impossible to create a living symbol, i.e., one that is pregnant with meaning, from known associations. (Jung, quoted in Jacobi 1971, 80)

Words, numbers, the emblem, the attribute, and the allegory (the laurel is the emblem of glory, the scale the attribute of justice, the winged woman the allegory for victory), as well as the metaphor and the analogy, are forms of verbal, mathematical, and pictorial expression that do not go beyond the level of signification (Chevalier and Gheerbrant 1973). They are imaginative or intellectual means of communication that point to something other than themselves, without stepping out of the realm of representation, and as such they are signs. "The symbol announces another level of consciousness than does rational evidence; it is the mark of a mystery, the single means for saying what cannot be otherwise apprehended" (Corbin, quoted in Chevalier and Gheerbrant 1973, xvi).

There are symbols that are lifeless, like envelopes with no contents. They do not have the power to inspire, nourish, and attract that living symbols have. They then degenerate to nothing but signs. The cross, for example, has for many become a simple sign of Christianity; it is for these people an extinguished symbol that has lost the richness and depth of its original meaning. A symbol is alive only as long as it is pregnant with meaning.

Signs are flat. One must go beyond their facade to rediscover the tridimensionality of symbols. It is the quality of how symbolic reality is viewed that makes it flat or alive, two- or three-dimensional. Closed off from access by our rational consciousness, symbols reveal themselves little by little when we approach them with sensitivity and an intuitive mind. Symbolic reality cannot be apprehended by merely rational thought only, for it simultaneously engages the mind, the senses, the feelings, and the intuition, addressing at once the whole being.

The Signifying Reading of Dreams

The quest for the meaning of symbols has been more or less important according to the dreams contained in each of the three dream series. All of Marjorie's dreams were dreams with symbolic contents. In Eric's series, however, the unfolding of outer and manifest activity dominated. Pierre's series came midway between the two other series in how it was centered on symbolic contents. In each series, certain dreams led to more elaborated amplifications. They appeared to be key dreams, and in the series studied they generally contained particularly powerful symbols.

In their original state, the dreams already contained everything. The difficulty for an unprepared reader, though, would have been to be in a position to "see" all that the dreams contained. My work has consisted in casting light on the dreams as if they were like texts that would have remained obscure for most people, and throwing into relief the inherent intelligence of the dream language of children, as well as the coherence and the esthetic power characterizing it.

This reading was meant to be as supple as possible. In certain cases, it has consisted only in "naming" the facts and gestures in a meaning-giving way; thus the motif of the rope surrounding the bed is "named" entanglement, the climb onto the mountain is ascension, the drowning followed by emergence is immersion and resurgence. In other cases, some elements were associated with one another: to entanglement was associated the labyrinth, to ascension the idea of verticality, to drowning the idea of descent. In still other cases, an interpretation of the meaning of a symbol was proposed: the ascension was interpreted as possibly expressing a release, the resurgence as expressing the manifestation of a rebirth. Naming, associating, explicating, and linking were done in order to put in relief the meaning and the coherence of the whole. Occasionally, certain symbols were amplified in strict accordance with the Jungian sense of the word *amplification*, whereby interpretations were associated to parallel contexts, brought forth and applied to the symbols in the dreams— for example, with the mandala and the engulfment symbols.

Some incoherencies have remained; some enigmas go unresolved. The series studied correspond to a brief moment in the vast movement of the dream life of their dreamers. A multitude of dreams has preceded the series, and considerable quantities will follow them. Each dream in each of these series appears as a wave crest, emerging to prominence in the consciousness of these children from the depths of a world that remains unknown to us.

Using Amplification with the Dreams of Children

Michael Fordham (1969) rightfully warns against "adultomorphic speculations" in the use of amplification with children's dreams. What is characteristic of an adult is then unfairly attributed to a child, and the analysis of dreams from the child's point of view is lost.

The advantage, however, of approaching children's dreams by considering the universal symbols within them is the dropping of barriers that too often separate the worlds of children and adults, thus causing us to recognize the deeply human dimension of children's dream experience. It has often been emphasized that symbolic language is a universal language insofar as it transcends the differences between cultures and times; the present study permits the view that symbolic expression also transcends age differences.

The amplification of the dream series that follow is theoretical rather than clinical in nature. In a clinical setting, amplifying dreams would assuredly take into consideration the personal universe of the dreamer. Exploring the context of the dream would first consist in obtaining the dreamer's subjective associations to the different elements of the dream in order to understand the subjective tissue to which the dream elements belong. But amplifying the dream could also consist in exploring beyond the personal universe of the dreamer through the universal symbolic heritage as expressed through time in art, poetry, and religion, to the deep and universal meaning of certain symbols that extend beyond the immediate reality of the dreamer and touch on the collective experience of humanity. Amplifying dreams would then become theoretical or objective.

The theoretical approach to dream amplification is especially convenient for research. It permits the consideration of symbolic language for its own sake. The intention of this work with children's dreams is not to conduct a clinical interpretation in terms of a particular psychological theory. In fact, no information about the personal lives of children was gathered. The task that awaits researchers, educators, and psychologists is first of all to recognize the validity and authentic weight of the dream language of children, and then to take the necessary steps in learning how to read the dreams of children in a faithful and meaningful way.

Furthermore, as Jung (1960) pointed out, children's dreams are often very rich in archetypal symbols, so that the symbols have roots that reach beyond the immediate and personal universe into what Jung called "the collective unconscious," and for which theoretical amplification is the only valuable method. Finally, children are unable to engage in the free-associative process (A. Freud 1974b; Jacobi 1971), which makes even more justifiable this recourse to an objective approach.

Dream interpretation raises the ethical problem of how to read and interpret the dreams of others without transgressing on the other's territory or encroaching on her or his personal life. Dreams express the ineffable; what is said in dreams is really said, and the gestures made in dreams are real gestures, in the same way that our thoughts are real acts that affect our lives. Some symbols require only that they be contemplated. And any too-hasty interpretation runs the risk of reducing symbols if not obscuring them. Dream amplification results from an encounter between the data and the researcher, and from this point of view amplification is also a creation in the sense of Carl Rogers's phrase "the emergence of a new product."

The interpretation of children's dreams requires that the researcher go beyond the clinical and often psychopathological framework where it first began; the theoretical and dynamic amplification may be a step in this direction.

Rendering the Children's Accounts of Dreams

The dreams have been rewritten in the third person and in the present time, in an effort to stay as close as possible to the child's original text and to the rhythm of the child's phrases. In their original version, certain texts of the dreams were confusing. Some details gained precision from one version to the next, and sometimes there were two and even three versions. Some of the dreams reported by the children were, however, of such limpidity and clarity that this rewriting of the original spoken protocol would not have been necessary. But in order to make the presentation of the dreams uniform, they have all been treated in the same way.

The purpose of this rewriting was to present a text that was intelligible and easy to read. The childlike grammatical forms have not been reproduced except within quotation marks. When details have been added to the initial version by the child—after the drawing was completed, for example—they have been identified as additions to the original version. Occasionally when the drawing of a dream led to its development or added a substantially significant dimension to it, the drawing has been described in full or in part. Otherwise, and in most cases, details from the drawings are included as part of the dream amplification.

Chapter Five

The Combat with the Monster

Each of the three series presented in Chapters 5, 6, and 7 portrays a particular mode of contact with the monster: combat, taming, and engulfment. Combat is the strategy most frequently used by dreamers as they encounter the monster. Threatened by the monster, children defend themselves and conceive a means of fighting the enemy. Combat is the way of the warrior-hero, and it is related to acquiring one's power or strength by conquest.

Eric's eight-dream series, reported over nine weeks, illustrates combat with the monster. The very first dream presents the problem of the monster, a problem that develops in subsequent dreams.

Dream One

Eric sleeps. It is night. There is a rope in front of his bed. He goes across his bed. Not across, he goes to the side. The rope prevents him from getting out of his bed. He goes to the other side. He returns to the back. He gets through and goes. And then there is a "huge enormous beast" that "is as tall as the sky" and a voice that says, "I smash the whole earth." Behind the monster there is a "big round" [hole]. The monster continues to walk. Eric sees the pieces of the earth dropping into the water. The monster takes the house and throws it into the water.

In retelling the dream after drawing it, Eric adds the detail that he was able to free himself from the back of his bed, where there was no rope, and get out into the rest of the house, where the monster was. He added that the monster saw him. The monster was looking at him and licking his lips as if to say, "That must be very good." Behind the monster the whole earth was falling into the water. Eric was watching this. He rushed back into the house, but before he could

43

escape, the monster took him in his jaws and threw him into the water. The monster came forward, "went over the earth," and then took the house and threw it into the water. In the drawing we see an image of Eric reflected in both eyes of the monster.

Amplification

The dream starts with Eric finding himself a prisoner in his own bed. There is a rope that blocks his way when he attempts to get out of his bed. Then he engages in movement as part of his search for an exit, involving much effort and many detours. This first scene suggests an entanglement, since the rope blocks Eric, and also evokes the myth of the walk in the labyrinth with its search for the center, because of the peregrinations entailed in finding his way that Eric describes.

Eric is confined. The rope restrains him within a limited space and he is thereby threatened with the prospect of remaining captive. But he reacts, beginning to disengage, and as he does so, he falls prey to a much larger danger, personified this time by a monster of immeasurable size that is going to shake the foundations of his universe in a scene that might be termed apocalyptic.

Eric describes how his whole world—the earth, his house, and himself—is violently buffeted by the monster. The destruction of the earth, the presence of the "beast," the prophetic tone of the voice that announces the event, and the rapid accumulation of symbols all suggest the apocalyptic character of the dream. The symbols thus accumulated are the sky, the earth, the water, the house, the monster, the mouth, the eyes, the voice, the return to water, and total destruction (see fig. 7).

Eric loses his underpinnings one after another. Neither earth nor house remains, and Eric is himself lifted off the ground by the monster, who takes him in his jaws and throws him into the water. There is a loss of contact with the earth, because it collapses and because Eric is lifted off it. Eric loses his first underpinning, the firm and security-giving earth, only to be thrown into the unknown and find himself at the mercy of an alien force he does not control.

Furthermore, it is the all-powerful monster that becomes the center of energy dominating this part of the dream. The house and the child are propelled to the periphery. The house is, among other things, a symbol for the center of the world and as such stands for the center of the universe of the child. In the present situation, the house momentarily loses its function as the center of direction and activity while under the domination of the energetic force that the monster represents. Thus Eric loses his second underpinning, the stable and reliable center for which the house stands.

The monster takes Eric into his mouth. The mouth is a living laboratory for transformation. But by contrast to the maternal womb, in which cells aggregate and multiply, the mouth is a place where food undergoes a process

Figure 7. Drawing 24" x 18". Through the window, on the second floor, Eric is in bed with the rope. On the ground are Eric, the monster, the earth in a state of destruction, and the water.

of being torn apart and dissolved. The fetus is on the evolving side of its life cycle, but chewed-up food is on its involuting side.

The involuting process signified by Eric's passage into the mouth of the monster has a parallel in the earth's movement of returning to the waters. These waters have such depth that the earth and the house can be engulfed in them. This engulfment by the waters indicates a return to origins. The idea of primordial waters is nearly universal. In Genesis the earth is separated from the waters; in Hindu tradition the earth is brought to the surface of waters by a diving animal, a boar; and a Shinto story tells of how heroes induced the earth to coagulate from water. Water precedes the organization of the cosmos, whereas the earth produces living forms. Water stands for the mass of all that is undifferentiated, whereas the earth represents the seeds of differentiated form (Chevalier and Gheerbrant 1973). In Eric's dream, the process is reversed. It is the earth that returns to the waters. Here there are two swallowings, one suggested by Eric's being taken into the monster's mouth and the other of the earth by the waters.

The dream begins with a state of inertia suggested by the images of the rope restraining Eric in bed and his painful walk in search of an exit, and then the dream shows a bursting into action with the sudden entrance of the monsters, followed by the double swallowing. The monster itself was watching Eric. It was watching him while licking its lips. It is as if Eric were devoured by the monster's gaze. J. E. Cirlot (1962) signals the importance of the dragon's gaze by noting its piercing and penetrating qualities. And he adds that the word *dragon* probably comes from the Greek *derkein*, which means "seeing." It is the beast's gaze that prompts Eric's attempt to escape.

In his drawing of the monster, Eric's image is reflected in both of the monster's two eyes. This creates an impression of blindness, as if the confusion caused by the monster's gaze was mirrored in the beast's eyes. Eric's image is within the eyes of the monster. In many traditional cultures, to have the image of someone is to exert a power over that person. There is also a literal basis for Eric's depiction, for closely gazing into the eyes of another shows one's own image reflected in each eye.

The voice that sounds is an unknown voice associated with the appearance of the monster, but it does not emanate specifically from it. This voice announces the disaster that will soon befall Eric's dream world.

The only strategy to which Eric has recourse is the attempt to escape at the moment when the monster directs its attention toward him, an attempt that fails, however, because the monster takes him in his jaws and throws him into the water.

Dream Two

> Eric is in bed when suddenly a monster enters his room. The monster is followed by two other monsters. The monsters throw everything onto the floor, but Eric wakes up and fights them. He drives them back into the fire. In the fireplace there is a "little triangle" that catches fire, and it burns the monsters, which then get out through the chimney.

Amplification

Again the monster appears in the domain of the child, although it has lost its apocalyptic and gigantic qualities. It is human-size and comes into the bedroom simply, by contrast to the sudden appearance of the monster in the preceding dream, an appearance that defied natural laws. But whereas it is alone in the first dream, here the monster is multiplied. Now there is not one but three monsters, all alike.

We witness the regressive multiplying of the monsters. And because of the deep symbolic content they embody, Eric's phantasmagorical monsters cannot be met directly. They require the use of magic, both the magic of the child's increased powers, for the child accomplishes the heroic task of forcing the monsters back into the fireplace, and the magic of the fire ignited by the amazing trick of the "little triangle."[1] The use of magic invests a person or an object with a power beyond its ordinary nature.

The monster of the first dream rendered any confrontation the child might make practically impossible. Breaking up the one gigantic monster into three monsters of more modest proportions is the first step in organizing the energy represented by the monsters. The overwhelming energy of the monster of the initial dream is shaped into more circumscribed forms.

Eric forces the three monsters back into the fireplace. He describes himself as if he were the one "who removes with magical ease those 'larger ones' who threaten his path, and instantly becomes himself the hero" (Wickes 1978, 60). Eric views himself as endowed with an idealized power in order to cope with the challenge the monsters present. This idealized power gives symbolic expression to the goal toward which Eric aims.

The fire works by magic in burning the monsters, which fly through the chimney into the air and then fall head-first toward the ground (see fig. 8). The presence of the triangle is sufficient for the lighting of the fire. Through his magical thinking, the child establishes a causal link between the two events. The triadic form occurs twice, first with the trio of monsters and then with the triangle, which is an agent of their destruction.

Dream Three

In the house there is a monster with whom Eric is closely linked in friendship. This monster, which is "the strongest in the whole world," is lying in bed with Eric. While the two friends are sleeping "straight as logs," two monsters enter their room. They take Eric's friend. But now all around Eric's bed the place is "full of monsters." The monsters say something by making signs. They go away. Eric wakes up. He awakens "Jos Lit" (the name of his monster friend):[2] "It is morning. It is time to wake up." Eric's mother is up. But Eric's friend has the power to disappear if someone besides Eric touches him—if "other monsters" or "other people" or "little babies" touch him. In this instance, Eric's monster friend "is done"; it disappears and immediately reappears next to Eric, then under Eric. When Eric's mother enters the room, she sees that Eric is on top of the monster. "What! There is a monster under you!" she says. Eric says, "Of course! There's always a monster under me."

Figure 8. Drawing 24" x 18". Through the bedroom window, on the left, Eric and the monsters can be seen. Through the living room window appears the chimney. The monsters are eliminated through the chimney.

Amplification

The creation of the imaginary companion, Eric's *alter ego* or double, was presaged by the double image of the child that the monster reflected back to him in the initial dream. From now on, Eric has an ally in his combat with the monsters, a being endowed with magical powers with whom Eric has a privileged link. Jos Lit's power to disappear makes him invulnerable. Hence his ultimate function in this dream is to protect Eric from the enemy monsters by standing in for Eric in the role of victim, a role soon reversed due to his indestructability. The two of them are untouchable.

The multiplication of monsters continues. In this dream, the monsters begin as two, and then they are a gang around the bed. These primitive monsters speak only in signs, but the content of their sign-speech remains unknown to us (Eric's voice became lower and finally indistinct as he spoke of this).

As the number of monsters increases, the child's recourse to a strategy of magic becomes refined. The magic power that Eric had attributed to himself is now displaced onto the imaginary companion, the "strongest in the whole world," and the fire-igniting power of the triangle is replaced by Jos Lit's more complex power to disappear. Here the magical powers concentrate in the imaginary companion.

Dream Four

Eric is in bed. He gets up. He walks. But there is a rope that stops him. Then he turns around. He falls onto his bed. And he starts sleeping again. He gets up again. He walks. He goes under the rope. He goes into the fireplace and sees a monster at the top of the chimney. The monster comes down and is followed by other monsters that also come. Then Eric's "monster friend" comes along, the one that "stays next to him," which Eric describes as "kind of small" but "kind of strong." And Jos Lit fights all of the other monsters.

The drawing shows these details: Jos Lit "shoots bullets into his body" in order to become "bigger and bigger." He knocks the monsters out and eats them.

Amplification

This dream recalls from the first dream the theme of the rope and of the painful walk in search of an exit. The image of peregrinations in the labyrinth suggested in the first dream becomes more specific here. The course Eric follows to free himself from imprisonment by the rope and reach the chimney consists in setting out, encountering the obstacle, turning around, collapsing into sleep, setting out again and walking, and overcoming the obstacle. Finally he arrives at the center, which the chimney represents, where he finds a monster followed by a horde of other monsters.

It is the imaginary companion who rescues Eric and takes charge of solving the problem for him. He intervenes from outside the house, whereas Eric has described himself as inside the house. The activity centered in Eric when he searches for an exit and attempts to free himself from the rope is now displaced upon the imaginary companion, and Eric becomes inactive. The pole of action moves from inside to outside, from Eric to his companion, from ego to other.

The imaginary companion "shoots bullets into his body" and he becomes "bigger and bigger." Jos Lit's preparation for facing the enemy monster and its cohort takes on its full meaning if we consider the symbolic significance of assimilating the metal that the bullets represent and the transformation that this process induces in Eric's ally. Eric's drawing shows that, using a machine gun, Jos Lit "shoots bullets into his body" by shooting them into the air and swallowing them. There is a second representation of Jos Lit, bigger this time, as he climbs onto the roof of the house. A third representation of Jos Lit shows him as he gets closer to the row of five monsters walking on the roof up to the chimney.

To eat bullets is tantamount to assimilating their energetic force and changing the aggressive power of bullets into an aggressive power at one's disposal, through digestion. And since bullets are metal, they also symbolize condensed and solidified cosmic energy (Chevalier and Gheerbrant 1973). Jung (1953) understands metal to refer to the "libido" in the form of vital energy and, more specifically, as sexual energy, because metal is subterranean. And according to Jung, the process of extraction of the quintessence of metal corresponds to the liberation of creative energy.

The absorption of bullets as conceived by Eric has the effect of transforming Jos Lit so he will be able to combat the monsters. In symbolic terms, the absorption of bullets might be equivalent to the active and creative mobilization of Eric's vital energy, so that he can face in a more dynamic way the challenge that the monsters present.

This dream marks a turning point. The ally moves from the victim's role to that of an aggressor. It is now Jos Lit who is transformed into a devouring monster, thus revealing himself in his strength. The apocalyptic monster of the first dream was a monster threatening to eat Eric; the engulfing water was swallowing his earth and his shelter. Here the situation has changed and balance is restored, because it is Eric by means of his ally who knocks, chews (Yes, Jos Lit has teeth!), and devours. The monsters disappear by being incorporated. Once eaten, the monsters are destroyed. And having been eaten, they reach the end of the regressive process that began with their multiplication.

By means of the imaginary companion, the child also assimilates the enemy monsters. The power of the monsters, which seemed terrifying at first, is symbolically appropriated by the child during the assimilation process, as if the assimilated monsters were integrated and thus vanquished. This is probably what leads Ernest Aeppli (1978) to say that parents can be certain that their child is on his or her way the day the child tells them: "I went into the forest. Then the wolf came, and I was very scared. But it did not eat me, it is I who ate it. And afterward my belly was all big" (71).

Dream Five

Eric goes on a walk with Pierre and Michel. The three encounter an elephant. "Pierre and Michel, get out of here!" says Eric to his two companions. Eric looks both ways and finds that they are nowhere to be found. Then Eric also flees. He goes to his house, where Pierre and Michel have gone, since they were both "of his family."

Amplification

For the first time, the monster appears as an animal instead of a phantasmagorical being. The appearance of the elephant marks a new development in the evolution of the form of energy that the monster represents. From being gigantic and single at first, the monster has been breaking down into a growing number of monsters and now becomes a single monster, but with the well-defined contours of an animal form.

Eric is with companions who are children like himself, whom he knows in waking life, by contrast to his imaginary friend.

Just as there is a change in the form the monster takes, there is a resumption of Eric's activity. He comes out of the inactivity that the previous dream had portrayed, for it was Jos Lit who had been deploying aggressive force against the enemy monsters. But here it is Eric who takes the initiative to sound the warning to his friends, who flee, and he is the last one to leave, which shows him as responsible for the group. In this dream the recourse to flight, which failed in the first dream, succeeds.

Dream Six

As Eric is going for a walk with Jos Lit, he sees an elephant "that was going along" and that "was eating everybody." The elephant eats Jos Lit, who disappears and then returns to his initial place. Eric continues and then notices a crocodile. But this crocodile is in a cage. Eric grabs Jos Lit. He "lifts him up into the air" and he throws him onto the other side of the river. Then Eric jumps to the other shore, takes a "big stone" and "throws" it onto the crocodile.

Amplification

The elephant reveals itself to be a devouring animal. Again we find the imaginary companion in the victim's role. And again Eric has recourse to the magical strategy of Jos Lit's disappearing and reappearing to cope with the situation. This situation recalls the situation in Dream Three, in which the enemy monsters had taken Jos Lit away when he was lying down next to Eric. Using his magical power, Jos Lit had disappeared and then returned to his place next to Eric. This harking back to a previous situation shows that the child's psychological development does not occur in a linear fashion, but progresses by forward leaps and momentary steps backward.

The crocodile appears as a new threat for the companions. But the danger presented by the crocodile is under more control due to its confinement within a cage.

Eric lifts Jos Lit into the air and throws him onto the other side of the river. Having placed his ally and himself out of danger, Eric arms himself with a stone, which he throws at the animal. It is Eric who now becomes the source of action, the protector of Jos Lit, and the aggressor against the crocodile with a stone, which, when whole, stands for unity and strength.

Jos Lit, who was shooting bullets into his body in an earlier dream, is now represented as a robot in Eric's drawing (see fig. 9). And the water, which swallowed Eric's world in the initial dream, here functions to Eric's advantage by separating Jos Lit and him from the crocodile.

Dream Seven

> Eric and Jos Lit are in their house. They are in bed when suddenly the house catches on fire, because a monster has pumped machine gun bullets into the house. Eric is not burned. He goes outside and extinguishes the fire with a hose. Jos Lit, though, is hurt by the fire, for Eric "hasn't had the time" (to save Jos Lit, one presumes, before hurrying out of the house to put out the fire).

Amplification

The monster takes on its phantasmagorical form again. But it remains singular, instead of multiplying as it had in Dreams Two, Three, and Four, and it has none of the immeasurable size of the monster in the first dream. The machine gun that had served to build up Jos Lit's power to confront the monsters earlier now serves the enemy against Eric and his companion. The fire, which has been Eric's magical help, now becomes the monster's weapon. The machine gun and the fire represent, like the water, forces that can at times help Eric and at times threaten him.

The monster attacks from the outside and with a machine gun. Earlier the monster was inside the house and more often in the child's bedroom. In the preceding dream, Eric was attacking the crocodile on the other side of the river using a stone. The strategies of the monster and of Eric resemble each other. Both intervene from a distance and use a weapon.

Here Eric's strategy consists in coping not with the monster directly but with his misdeeds. Eric extinguishes the fire with a hose. The water, which has immersed Eric in the beginning, is an element that becomes increasingly advantageous to him. It becomes in Eric's hand a means to fight the fire, as if Eric had appropriated for himself a bit of the potency of water during his immersion.

For the first time, Jos Lit is hurt. He is no longer "the indestructible one" of the earlier dreams. He is more like the child in his vulnerability. And Eric takes more and more responsibility for Jos Lit, the hurt one. Eric himself is not burned. He is in charge of the situation. So far we have seen the center of action pass from Jos Lit as a powerful defender of Eric to Eric as respon-

Figure 9. Drawing 12" x 5". Jos Lit, the robot monster. On his right, the elephant. Higher from left to right: Eric and Jos Lit, the river, Eric and the crocodile.

sible for Jos Lit. In the earlier dreams Jos Lit served as a substitute for Eric in the victim's role, then became Eric's active defender, and now Eric can exercise his own strength when Jos Lit is hurt.

Dream Eight

Eric goes for a walk with Jos Lit. They come to a waterfall. Eric slides toward the bottom of the waterfall. He falls through the water and arrives in a pipe. But the waterfall does not push him far enough to get him to the exit. And by himself he is incapable of moving. In spite of this, they were "strong." Then Jos Lit, whose feet were still in the waterfall, slides like Eric. He enters the pipe. Their feet are like "two engines" behind them at that moment, and having thus "more strength," they move forward.

Amplification

The two allies undergo the same trial, and it is in coordinating their resources that they get through. There is a rapport of equality between the two, and each of them exerts an active force interdependently. The relationship between the two appears in a new light. Beyond the roles of mutual protection observed up until now, the two allies meet through the medium of their conjoined forces.

This dream brings to mind the scene of immersion in water of the initial dream. The child here loses his foothold and is again thrown into the water, the power of which draws him toward the unknown. But the water is not so deep here, and the outcome, which remained uncertain in the first dream, becomes clear in this one. The descent stops and the movement of Eric and his companion can go forward again. The two companions are propelled by a force coming from their feet, which suggests a regained power, if we consider that in the first dream Eric had lost his underpinnings when he was thrown into the void by the monster.

Immeasurably powerful at first, the monster reappears in the form of a growing number of phantasmagorical beings: one monster accompanied by two others, two monsters and a whole gang, one monster followed by a horde of others. The initial mass of energy, then, has broken down into many forms and is reorganized as a monster in animal form.

Parallel to this development, the coping strategies evolve through attempts to escape, recourse to the magic of the little triangle and its more sophisticated form, which is the imaginary companion. The relationship between child and imaginary companion progresses also. At first, Jos Lit substitutes himself for Eric in the role of victim. But his magic power renders him indestructible. Then Jos Lit becomes the powerful defender of Eric, attacking and devouring all the enemy monsters. Liberated, Eric gradually regains his own power. He is then able to be the responsible one as Jos Lit becomes more and more vulnerable. In the end, the two companions have a relationship that has grown into a new form of association beyond mutually protective roles. They join forces in a new rapport based on equality.

Jos Lit, "the strongest in the whole world," compensates for the weakness of Eric, who is overcome by the first monster. Jos Lit, endowed with magic powers, protects Eric from the monsters who threaten him during his dreams. Jos Lit, aggressor and devourer, dares to do what Eric fears to do, and serves as a model for Eric, who gradually frees his own energetic force.

Chapter Six

The Taming of the Monster

By contrast to combat, taming the monster is a much rarer occurrence in children's dream life. But taming is extremely rich in what it teaches. It pertains to the domain of the heart.

Pierre's eleven-dream series[1] reported over ten weeks portrays the use of taming in the encounter with the monster. The first two dreams of the series, both told during the first interview, put Pierre on the scene with the character of the monster and with his mother. This triangular relationship develops through the series.

Dream One

Pierre is in his bed. He hears a noise (wheet, wheet, wheet). He looks through the window. There is nothing there. He goes downstairs. He still finds nothing. He returns upstairs. He wonders what is happening. There was some small thing downstairs. In retelling the dream, after drawing it, he refers to "a kind of bug" downstairs.[2] Pierre touches it. The thing is "through his hand." He also explains after drawing the dream that he could see his hand "through" the bug and that in contact with the bug his hand "became all red." Pierre pulls his hand out. He notes that he could do that. He wonders what it is.

Then he looks through the window and notices that there is a flying saucer landing. During the retelling of the dream, after he has made his drawing, Pierre introduces the following variant: he looks through the window and he notices that the bug makes him blind. He adds that this is what happened when one put one's hand through it. In his drawing, Pierre represents the bug as a small mass drawn in red, through which the imprint of his hand shows, also in red.

55

Amplification

Pierre is led toward the unknown by an unfamiliar sound that prompts him to look for its origin. He searches the house from top to bottom. He looks through the window. His first move is to trace the source of the sound that triggers his curiosity. Finally, downstairs he finds something like a small mass, judging from his drawing of the bug, through which his hand shows (see fig. 10). Pierre's spontaneous impulse is to touch the unknown thing. He pushes his whole hand into it. He explores what is unknown by direct contact. When he pulls his hand out, it has changed. It has become red.

Pierre returns to the window after withdrawing his hand from the bug. At first he refers to the arrival of the flying saucer as if there was a link between the strange creature that he finds in the house and the arrival of the spaceship. Three unusual events follow one another: the advent of the sound, the discovery of the strange bug, and the arrival of the flying saucer. Each event in its own way points to the entrance of something unknown into Pierre's world, arouses his curiosity, and prompts his active search for and exploration of the unknown.

In his second telling of the dream episode in which he returns to the window after having touched the bug, Pierre refers to the blindness that the unknown creature causes him. The blindness suggests some confusion in Pierre and connotes a loss of power, the power of vision, which is associated with a loss of consciousness.

Dream Two

Pierre is in bed. He comes downstairs, where he sees Suzie. He wonders what is happening, since she is with his mother in the middle of the night. He goes upstairs. He watches his mother, who is lying in bed.

In the drawing there is a large insect above the mother, whom we see lying in bed. The insect has many legs, proboscises, antennae, and wings. While he is drawing, Pierre comments: "This is to catch the small things and the big things. This picks up all the blood. More and more! Look, my mother lacks blood." After his drawing, he identifies the insect: "It is a bug and it takes back the blood." As for him, Pierre watches this and rushes to escape.

Amplification

Pierre gets up during the night and is astonished to find his younger sister downstairs with his mother at this late hour. He returns upstairs and sees his mother lying in her bed. In the drawing showing the development of the dream, there is a vampire-insect that draws blood out of Pierre's mother. Pierre witnesses this scene and hurries to escape (see fig. 10).

Figure 10. Drawing 24" x 18". Left side: window, Pierre in his bed, hand print in the bug. Right side: the insect drawing blood. In the bed, Pierre's mother.

While he is drawing this dream, there is a moment when Pierre enters the character of the vampire-insect. He describes the function of the bug's organs: "This picks up all the blood." He penetrates to the very heart of the action, momentarily, as if he had become the vampire-insect that draws blood: "more and more." At this instant there is an intensification of his presence in the action. Pierre animates the character, which becomes alive and acts in an astonishing manner. He leaves the narrative and plunges into the action, drawing the blood and noticing the results: "Look, my mother lacks blood."

The dream sets the stage for the Pierre-mother-monster triangle. The monster attacks the mother. Pierre witnesses the scene. The triangle collapses for a moment into a duality when Pierre jumps into the role of the vampire-insect. At that instant, the conflict is polarized between the child-vampire-insect and the mother.

The vampire gives form to an unconscious content. Erich Neumann (1972) associates the vampire with the archetype of the Terrible Mother,[3] an archetype being a pattern of psychic energy, both ancient and universal. The vampire-insect of Pierre's dream recalls among other figures the Stryges of Greek mythology, winged female demons with the talons of birds of prey who feed on the blood and entrails of children (Oriol-Boyer 1975). In Dream Two the monster drains the vital energy of Pierre's mother. It is as if, through a substitution of roles, the child imagines his mother in the victim's position when he enters the character of the monster, which he fears. Identifying with the monster can be a way of beginning to integrate into oneself what it represents.

When Pierre identifies with the vampire-insect, the scene takes on for an instant the characteristics of a power struggle between Pierre and his mother. Under cover of the vampire-insect, Pierre becomes the aggressor, drawing the blood of the victim-mother. Drawing the blood of a witch, de Vries (1974) observes, is equivalent to breaking her or his power, and the one who draws the blood of a witch becomes immune to the witch's power.

Pierre comes out of the character of the vampire-insect and again becomes the outside witness to the scene involving the blood-drawing insect and his own mother. He hurries to escape as if frightened or embarrassed by the scene he has been watching.

The red color appearing in the previous dream and the blood in the vampire-insect dream suggest a continuity in the theme of red and blood, and a relationship between the bug that makes Pierre's hand red and the vampire-insect.

Dream Three

> Pierre gets up during the night. He pours water into his shoes and a monster appears.

Amplification

Like the vampire-insect, this monster has antennae and proboscises. Otherwise, its form resembles the human form, except that it has no arms. The identical attributes of the vampire-insect and of the monster in this dream reveal a relationship between the two. The monster with which Pierre has momentarily identified in the previous dream is here literally in his shoes.

What the dream shows clearly is that it is Pierre himself who through his action gives rise to the creation of the monster. He creates it when he pours the water into his shoes. The medium through which the monster arrives is water, a fluid and mobile element that can take all possible forms.

Dream Four

Pierre is in his bed. He sees threads that move around. He watches them. He touches them and they form balls. When he begins touching them again, they form shapes "like head shapes." He begins to touch them and they make "all sorts of things," and then "a big monster." Pierre goes outside. He climbs on the car. When the monster touches water, he dies. And his blood creates another monster.

Amplification

Through his touch, Pierre transforms unaccustomed objects that present themselves to his eyes. With each new contact, the unknown gains in precision of form. From threads, it becomes balls, and from balls it becomes heads, and after another transformation, it becomes a monster. Again, by doing these things, Pierre has created a monster so large that Pierre flees.

At first it is Pierre who approaches the unknown and who transforms it. Then it is the monster who is in control and who gets Pierre to flee. Pierre presses forward with his actions until he can no longer cope with the phenomenon he has provoked. At this moment he escapes. His attitude is audacious initially and almost experimental. He explores the unknown by acting on it and by observing the effect of his action. He retreats when what he provokes has become larger than he. The monster who was attacking Pierre's mother at the beginning of the dream series now turns against Pierre.

The hand pushed into the bug and made red in Dream One is now endowed with the power to metamorphose objects, as if it had a vital force at its disposal. Pierre is saved from the monster by the action of the water, which has the power to make the monster die. One imagines the monster becoming water again, melting just as we had seen it emerge from the water poured into Pierre's shoes in Dream Three. There is a twofold function of the water in the series, which both creates the monster and annihilates it.

From the blood of the dead monster a new monster is born. The red, the blood, and the water continue to be associated with the monster as the series unfolds. In India, water is considered the preserver of life as the element that flows through all of nature in the form of rain, sap, milk, and blood (Cirlot 1962). In the context of this dream series, water and blood seem to partake of the same fundamental nature.

Dream Five

Pierre is lying in bed. He sees something like blocks, which move by. He takes them and goes to show them to his mother, who tells him, "Throw this outside." Now, these blocks could not be put out in the cold or they would become like the Blob. Pierre explains that the Blob is a movie character that his brother has seen on television. It is a red liquid that must be kept in the freezer. If it is taken out of the cold, it changes into the Blob. The Blob eats everybody, and the more it eats, the bigger it becomes. Pierre's mother throws the blocks into the cold, outside into the snow. And the liquid changes into the Blob. Pierre goes to tell his mother to put the thing back into the freezer. She puts it back and Pierre goes to tell his brother that it is the first time he has seen this.

Amplification

From one dream to the next, the monster moves closer and closer to Pierre, emerging in Pierre's shoes, scaring Pierre into fleeing, and now threatening to eat him.

The frozen red liquid that has the power to create the monster combines the symbolic meanings of water and blood already associated with the creation of the monster in Dreams Three and Four. It is also associated with the vampire-insect of Dream Two because of the blood and with the bug that reddened Pierre's hand in the initial dream.

The dynamic among Pierre, mother, and monster develops. Until now it has been Pierre who through his actions has contributed to the creation of the monster. But here it is Pierre's mother who throws the blocks outside, leading to the animation of the monster. His mother moves from the position of the victim in Dream Two to the one who prompts the monster to come forth.

Safety is restored when the blocks from which the Blob emerges are put back into the freezer by Pierre's mother. The mother here is in the role of an adult ally of the child. It is Pierre, though, who knows how to proceed in order to control the monster and who guides his mother in her actions. Pierre and his mother unite their forces against the monster. The antagonistic relationship shown in the vampire-insect dream here changes into a cooperative one.

The monster is controlled. It is not destroyed or killed, but contained. That is, the monster is brought down to a size that is no longer threatening.

The character of the brother in the series appears for the first time in Dream Five. He is the one who first saw the Blob in a film on television and he is the one to whom Pierre says with astonishment that this is the first time he has ever seen such a phenomenon as the Blob.

Dream Six

Pierre dreams that he goes with his brother to Pohénégamouk. His brother sees someone who is outside the train and who puts "some rocks" on the tracks of their train where the wheels run. They have an accident. They survive it, however. They leave the train. They follow the rails and go to the train station.

Amplification

This dream breaks from the theme of the phantasmagorical monster and from the creative exploration of the previous dreams. The brother to whom the Blob dream referred appears again in the role of Pierre's traveling companion. Just as Pierre's older brother had first seen the Blob on television and had given Pierre an account of his experience of the Blob phenomenon, so this same brother first sees the mysterious person who puts rocks on the rails and causes the derailing. In both situations it is the brother who sees before Pierre sees.

The accident is a disaster, but Pierre and his brother survive it: "It is we who succeed in living," says Pierre, who describes himself and his brother as if they were the objects of especially good fortune. The accident occurs on the railway tracks leading to Pohénégamouk. The two brothers are back to normal with the return to the train station.

Dream Seven

Pierre dreams that he falls off a building. He and his brother were walking with their eyes closed. Pierre felt heavy. When he opened his eyes, he found himself on the edge of the building. His brother startles him and he falls.

Amplification

The accident is followed by the fall off the building. The two brothers walk with their eyes closed. The heaviness Pierre feels gives him a numb sensation. When Pierre opens his eyes, he discovers that he is on the edge of a precipice, from which, startled by his brothers, he falls.

Walking with eyes closed on the roof of a building suggests a blindness in Pierre, who seems to grant a certain absolute trust to his brother. In the last two dreams, the brother was seeing the dangers before Pierre spotted them, but here Pierre's trust in his brother leads to his fall from the roof. The drawing of the dream shows Pierre in free fall in a position perpendicular to the wall of the building (see fig. 11). There seems to be a trick used by the older brother, since it is in startling Pierre that he provokes the fall, as if the brother "played with" Pierre's "blind trust," leading Pierre to fall victim to his lack of discrimination.

The fall to the bottom of the building, a building drawn like a tower, corresponds to a movement from the heights to the ground. Pierre finds himself on the earth, which is to say in contact with reality, and in this sense dreams of falling often are occasions for insight.

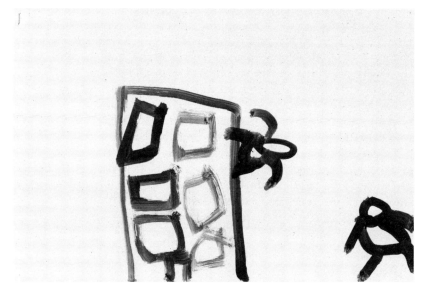

Figure 11. Drawing 18" x 12". Pierre is shown falling off the building and then on the ground after his fall.

Dream Eight

Pierre sees a crocodile. Instead of running away, he tries to stroke it. When he pets the crocodile, the crocodile "grows smaller." Pierre brings it to his mother and shows it to her. He asks her if he may keep it. His mother says, "If he is gentle." The crocodile "is gentle" and they keep it.

Amplification

The dream of the crocodile brings the problem of the monster and of the Pierre-mother-monster triangle back to the surface. But for the first time, the monster is a known animal. All the others belonged to the order of phantasmagorical beings. This monster has a well-defined animal nature and it appears in the child's bedroom.

Instead of running away from the crocodile, Pierre chooses to move toward it and attempts to pet it. In response to Pierre's movement of affection, the animal is transformed. The crocodile's transformation is of two kinds: first there is a change in size, since the animal gets smaller. Second, the crocodile is changed from a wild and ferocious animal into an animal so "gentle" that the child is allowed to keep him. "Whoever is incapable of love will be incapable of transforming [the dragon] and things will follow their ancient course," notes Jung (1962, 335; translated by the author).[4]

Pierre's move toward the crocodile points to the power of the heart, solely capable of transforming the dragon. The absence of fear that characterizes the encounter between Pierre and the crocodile is a privilege of the innocence of childhood: "Only the child without malice, the man without mistrust, cannot be frightened by the presence of the serpent. All other humans experience deep terror toward it. This is one of the secrets of childhood that vanishes with it: in growing up, the individual forgets about the totality of childhood, about the child who knows how to let a whole world live within himself, without paralyzing it with reflections, judgments and condemnations, and about the child who lives in a kind of Garden of Eden where all beings prosper peacefully next to one another" (Jung 1962, 320; translated by the author).

It is with his bare hands and without weapons that Pierre approaches the animal. Pierre's hand, which plunged into the "bug" at the beginning of the series and turned red, and which transformed the unusual objects, now knows how to tame. Pierre is by himself when he tames the monster. This encounter is a face-to-face meeting between Pierre and the monster, an ultimate moment when nothing and no one interferes.

Pierre brings the tamed crocodile to his mother and shows it to her. Then he asks her permission to keep it. Pierre brings the fruit of his conquest to his mother as if to receive her recognition. His mother receives him and assents to his request to keep the animal. The Pierre-mother-monster triangle reaches a point of balance. Pierre, his mother, and the monster are in harmony (see fig. 12).

Pierre's taming strategy is of a nonviolent nature and has a subtle power that disarms and transforms rather than attacks and destroys. The taming of the crocodile and the point of balance reached in this dream come after the awakening caused by the pivotal incident of falling off the building.

Dream Nine

Pierre is in bed. He sees a small animal. The animal sticks out its tongue and Pierre sees that it is a snake. He grabs it, "it was a small baby." Pierre brings it to his mother to tell her that it is a snake. But the mother says that it is "only a garden snake." Pierre wants to keep it. And they keep it. Later Pierre relates that when he took the animal into his arms, he felt a chill. Pierre's mother was not afraid, since for her the snake was small.

Figure 12. Drawing 18" x 12." The crocodile's metamorphosis: the crocodile before and after its transformation, Pierre's mother, Pierre.

Amplification

This dream seems to be a replay of the scenario of the previous dream, as if the child was repeating the outlines of the story as a means of better integrating the event of the taming that he experienced spontaneously and for the first time in the dream of the crocodile.

The animal that Pierre confronts in this dream is a "baby." Nevertheless, it gives Pierre a chill when he takes it into his arms. But it is not a challenge on the same scale as the crocodile and the other monsters seen earlier. And the mother does not perceive Pierre's deed as so valorous a conquest, since the challenge represented by a garden snake is not on the same scale as that of the crocodile. The animal monster has regressed to infant form.

The rapport between child and monster, which had reached a point of balance in the dream of taming the crocodile, here swings over in favor of the child as the monster is infantilized.

Dream Ten

Pierre dreams that he is in bed and that everything moves. He throws a glass of water and there is someone who appears, a being who changes into all sorts of colors. Pierre decides to touch it and this stops.

Amplification

This dream recalls the problem of the phantasmagorical monster and resolves it. We again meet all the elements of Pierre's oneiric world observed so far: the objects in the space of his room, the monster that forms as a result of his action, and the water as a medium for the emergence of the monster. The monster is in perpetual transformation; it takes on all sorts of colors. Pierre dispels it with his touch, just as he had tamed the crocodile with his touch. Pierre's strategy clearly implies a constant use of the power of his hand, the red hand that creates, transforms, tames, and now dispels the phantasmagorical monster.

Dream Eleven

Pierre is in a store with his brother. He plays "a lot of dirty tricks" on the store. There is a "lady with a kind of mirror." The mirror makes a noise. When she "lights up" people with her mirror, they go away. They are afraid. Pierre wakes up and goes to lay in bed with his mother, and he is afraid. Pierre had lost track of his brother. He explains later: the lady "had hit him [Pierre] with the sun." She had touched Pierre with it. When she touched people, they went away. Once they were outside the store, they fainted. He woke up.

Amplification

After taming the crocodile, and after dispelling the phantasmagorical monster, there arises a new dream character whose power succeeds in provoking Pierre's awakening. So far we have seen the threatening dream character evolve from phantasmagorical monster to the animal and now to the human and female form of the woman with the mirror. The unconscious psychic content that the monster represents is embodied in more and more concrete and realistic forms. The problem of the monster unfolds as it manifests itself in the consciousness of the child-dreamer.

The unknown woman is endowed with a mirror, a feminine and lunar symbol, since the mirror, like the moon, reflects light without being itself a source of light. Pierre plays "a lot of dirty tricks" as the woman with the mirror appears. Pierre describes himself as doing something reprehensible: the drawing shows a gum machine, the glass of which he has broken. The functions of the mirror enable a seeing and a revealing. Furthermore, to direct a mirror toward the sun in order to see suggests a divinatory procedure. Indeed, certain shamans practice divination by means of a mirror, directing it toward the sun or the moon, which are also considered mirrors reflecting what happens on earth (Chevalier and Gheerbrant 1973). Hence one is led to believe that the woman with the mirror "sees." She uses her mirror by "lighting up" people, which instills fear in them and leads to their removal. Thus the initiative of the guilty Pierre falls under the gaze of the woman with the mirror.[5]

Insofar as it catches the solar fire, the mirror is also often considered a solar symbol. There is a destructive power associated with the mirror manipulated by the woman in Pierre's dream. In one of his drawings, Pierre represented a large sun; from a large ray of the sun a black fire was reaching down to a smoking form on the ground. Pierre commented on his drawing as follows: "The sun makes big rays, to make a big fire. . . because there were maniacs, and the sun had decided to kill them. He [the maniac] had caught a little boy, and the sun had killed him." From the sun's rays, the destructive fire was born. The fire killed the maniac that threatened the child. In this dream the woman catches the solar power by means of her mirror and directs it against the child. The same solar force that was on the child's side in the drawing works here to his detriment.

According to Pierre's expression, the woman with the mirror "hits people with the sun" and she causes the fainting of those whom she touches. Fainting stands for a loss of consciousness and it recalls the blindness that Pierre experienced when he touched the strange creature in the first dream of the series. In both cases, Pierre's initiative results in some kind of loss of consciousness. Finally, the mirror, which makes a noise, echoes the unusual sound that had set Pierre on the track of the unknown at the very beginning of the series.

Pierre has lost his brother when he is touched by the rays from the woman's mirror. He is without the protection of his companion in adventure and thus alone facing this situation. Those who are touched by the rays of the mysterious woman faint when they come out of the store. But Pierre himself does not faint. Again we find a sense of special protection or natural good luck, which had already saved Pierre in the train accident of the earlier dream. Pierre wakes up and takes refuge in his mother's bed.

In the dream, the situation polarizes between Pierre and the woman with the mirror. Just as the vampire-insect went largely beyond the personal mother[6] because of the deep unconscious content that it embodied, so the woman with the mirror, who perhaps breaks off like a shadowy double from the personal mother, also goes beyond her. The woman with the mirror is the mysterious unknown female appearing in a public place, and her rays affect not only Pierre but also the other "people."

The mirror of the unknown woman, due to its solar character, suggests creative intelligence and magical power, and as such it reflects Pierre's creative magic, under whose touch the monster emerged, transformed, and was dispelled.

The dream of the woman with the mirror is a key dream in this series insofar as it makes more explicit and clarifies the many facets of the relationship between Pierre and his mother, Pierre and the feminine, and Pierre and the monster.

The first dreams of Pierre's series are characterized by a brisk activity: Pierre searches, touches, explores, inhabits, and creates the monster. At the heart of the unfolding of Pierre's activity, there is his hand, plunged into the strange red "bug" at the very beginning of the series and endowed with the power of transforming, taming, and dispelling the monster. The dream character Pierre is revealed in his vulnerability with the dreams of the accident and of the fall. And when unexpectedly the woman with the mirror arrives, it is too much for Pierre. The threatening dream character, for its part, evolves from the phantasmagorical form to the animal form and then to the human form.

As soon as the point of balance is attained with the dreams of the taming and the dispelling, after the intense creative exploration of the first dreams and beyond the pivotal dreams of the accident and the fall, a new challenge arises with the appearance of the woman with a mirror, and we leave the series on a suspended note.

Chapter Seven

The Engulfment by the Monster

If combat is the most frequent way of encountering the monster, and if taming is the richest in what it teaches, then engulfment is certainly the most paradoxical. Engulfment partakes of the mysteries of death and rebirth.

Marjorie's eleven-dream series, which extends over ten weeks, illustrates engulfment by the monster. The odyssey of Marjorie is a passage through the belly of the whale and after. This series follows the progress of Marjorie through her descent and resurgence.

Dream One

In Marjorie's dream, her friend Caroline stays overnight at her house. There is "a large baby carriage" on which Marjorie can "embark." And her friend Caroline pushes the carriage when Marjorie is in it. Marjorie and her friend see a monster. Marjorie wakes up. She tells the dream to her father. Her brother is there on the couch. He is not afraid. She returns to bed and does not think about it anymore.

Amplification

Marjorie climbs into a baby carriage that is large enough for her. In climbing into this vehicle, she prepares to go somewhere, although the destination is not indicated. But she is not in charge of driving the carriage that conveys her. Caroline, a child her age who is her friend, is in charge. Caroline generates and orients the movement while Marjorie offers no resistance. At first, departing in the baby carriage seemed like a harmless enterprise, but when the monster comes, departing in the carriage seems to be the beginning of an adventure. In Marjorie's drawing, the monster is represented as an animal.

The baby carriage is a symbol of the center, since it is a modern form of the chariot. This suggests that Marjorie is psychologically at the center, which is to say that Marjorie is in contact with the trust of an inner energy symbolized by the movement of the vehicle.

The baby carriage Marjorie occupies is a vehicle for small children. Marjorie's drawing shows that this baby carriage has high handles in back. Marjorie, in the baby carriage, has put herself in the position of a young child, like a baby being strolled, when the monster appears.

Being strolled in the baby carriage entails the idea of movement. And the "embarking" on it suggests getting into a boat, a "bark," and journeying in this boat. Thus Marjorie undergoes two kinds of movement—one horizontal and in space, which strolling the baby carriage stands for, and one vertical and in time, since Marjorie identifies with the situation of a baby.

Marjorie awakens and tells her dream to her father while her brother is present. It strikes her that her brother is not afraid. She goes back to bed and lets the dream leave her thoughts.

Dream Two

Marjorie is outside, close to "a rail" where the trains go. She plays on it. She hears the whistle of a train...the train is getting closer to her. She stays where she is. She thinks it will "turn aside." But it smashes into her. An ambulance comes up the road. The men in the ambulance see her and pick her up, and she goes to the hospital.

Amplification

Marjorie is the victim of an accident as she is playing on the railroad tracks. In her drawing, she shows the tracks as long and narrow, running horizontally from one end of the paper to the other. The railroad tracks evoke the taking of a journey like the "embarking" in the baby carriage of the previous dream.

Marjorie is playing with a ball. Her drawing shows her arms up with the ball high over her head. The ball is drawn with a circle divided by a diagonal cross, like a *mandala*. Rhoda Kellogg (1969), a researcher who analyzes children's art, makes the following observation: "Mandalas made by children are often Combines, formed of a circle or a square divided into quarters by a Greek cross or a diagonal cross, or Aggregates, formed of a circle or a square divided into eighths by the two crosses together" (64).

Mandala is the Sanskrit word for circle. In her essay on symbolism in the visual arts, Aniela Jaffé (1964) says that the mandala, often a circle with four or eight rays, is found in ancient and modern architecture: in the layouts of houses, temples, palaces, fortresses, and cities; in the religious art of the East and of the West. This configuration is present in the rosettes of cathedrals, in the halos of saints (divided into four in the Christian tradition), in the circular patterns that serve to support meditation in the Orient, squares oriented with four doors and containing circles or lotuses populated by sacred beings and symbols, in spaces traced on the ground for rites of initiation, in creation myths positing the center as the place of the creation of the world.

The mandala appears in the early drawings of children, and also in the architecture, art, and religious rites and myths of adults everywhere, constituting a link between the expression of the child and that of the adult. As a circle, the mandala is a center for emergence, a point where axes converge, and it is a universal symbol for the center. This mandala, according to von Franz (1964), is "a symbolic representation of 'the nuclear atom' of the human psyche whose essence we do not know" (213). According to Jung (1972), the mandala tends to appear in pictures and in dreams of people during periods of inner conflict. The mandala has a compensating and regulating function, pointing toward a new integration of the personality.

In modern symbolism, a train often stands for a snake or a dragon. A powerful and anonymous mass coming into view from the unknown, the train glides on railroad tracks with the fluidity and undulating motion of the snake. The advent of this powerful vehicle in Marjorie's dream expresses a sudden eruption of energy of great force that knocks her down with sufficient violence to smash her. In a brusque and violent way, Marjorie enters into contact with the energy that the train represents and that recalls the monster she had escaped by waking up from the preceding dream.

Marjorie hears the whistle of the train announce its coming. She sees it approaching, but she does not move, since she thinks that the train is going to "turn aside." Even though she is aware of the oncoming train, Marjorie seems to believe she is out of danger, or else she is unconscious of the danger that the train represents for her. And then the train hits her. She gets help from the ambulance men who see her, pick her up, and take her to the hospital.

Dream Three

Marjorie dreams that she goes by car to the ocean and that she drowns. Then she sees a whale and a shark. The whale eats her.

In her drawing, Marjorie pictures herself in the belly of the whale. Her head is down, and she is surrounded with green matter that represents the entrails of the monster.

Amplification

Again the dream opens with the theme of movement. Marjorie goes by car to the ocean. Marjorie's adventure continues. This time her movement takes her to the vast and open space that nature and the ocean stand for, placing this dream under the sign of water.

The vehicle in which Marjorie travels this time is not a baby's conveyance but an adult one, and Marjorie seems to be the driver, since she is by herself and the dream does not refer to other people present. Surprising as it may be, children who have only had the experience of riding as passengers in automobiles readily imagine themselves at the wheel in their dreams, notes Patricia Garfield (1984).

Vehicles that appear in dreams are always derivative of the essential symbol of the chariot. In several traditions, including Plato's, the chariot and its horse-and-driver arrangement have been compared to the human body and the emotional and intellectual functions. The driver thus stands for the inner center of direction in the person. The chariot, and car, stand for the body, a vehicle for the life of the human being, and here of Marjorie.

To summarize the scenario of the dream, Marjorie is in a car that she drives to the ocean. She leaves this vehicle and enters into the water, where for a moment she is bare of a bodily enclosure. She is handed over to the motions of the fluid and finally gets to the belly of the whale as if entering another bodily enclosure that will serve her as a temporary vehicle.

The theme from the first dream of returning in time continues in this dream. Marjories drowns and then is engulfed by the whale. We see her, upside-down, surrounded by green matter representing the entrails of the whale (see fig. 13).

The return to a previous time, which in the dream of the baby carriage took Marjorie back to early childhood, continues here into a past far more remote, to the time when Marjorie, still a fetus, was in the maternal womb, symbolized by the belly of the whale. But the whale is more than a maternal belly, since it is a symbol of the world itself. Thus we are led to believe that Marjorie implants herself in a womb far different from the maternal womb. It is a much larger vessel that navigates at a much greater depth and that bears within itself the possibility of birth into a world also larger, with a renewed consciousness.

Before being engulfed by the whale, Marjorie drowns. This suggests a moment of passage from one state of consciousness to another, after which she seems to be endowed with the capacity for another discernment, since at that moment she sees the sea monsters, the whale and the shark. Since Marjorie can see the whale and the shark, we might infer that the water in her dream is clear rather than in turmoil or tumult. Marjorie seems to offer no resistance to the process she undergoes, as if she had surrendered to it, protected by the

Figure 13. Drawing 18" x 12". The engulfment by the whale. Pictured are the car, the ocean, and Marjorie surrounded by the entrails of the whale.

innocence that characterizes childhood. Adults, more attached to themselves, are more likely to resist and struggle and to find themselves handed over to a stormy sea, as Jonah was.

Marjorie passes through water before coming into the belly of the whale. This suggests that the process she undergoes includes a kind of dissolution, a dissolution of the boundaries of herself into the infinite immensity of the ocean. For Erich Neumann (1970), the return to the ocean is an expression of return to the uroboric and undifferentiated consciousness, which characterizes prenatal life and the very beginnings of all existence: "The phase in which the ego is contained in the unconscious, like the embryo in the womb, when the ego has not yet appeared as a conscious complex, and there is no tension between the ego system and the unconscious, is the phase we have designated as uroboric and pleromatic" (276).

The emergence of the ego and of consciousness occurs gradually while the ego's tendency to dissolve back into the unconscious persists. The two tendencies function like opposite and dynamic polarities. Regression toward uroboric consciousness and fixation at this first level of consciousness occupies an important part of the life of the average person, notes Neumann (1970). This regression might be either neurotic and destructive or progressive and creative.

From Neumann's perspective, Marjorie's return to the ocean signifies a return to the original uroboric consciousness. Marjorie returns to water as if returning to the first element of her existence as a fetus. She returns to her place of origin.

The engulfment by the whale and the entrance into the belly of the whale evoke the mysteries of death and rebirth. In certain locales, the initiatory rites of puberty require entry into a mannequin that looks like an aquatic monster (crocodile, whale, or big fish). On the occasion of the child's initiation, the child is introduced into the belly of the monster. The pregnant monster later gives birth to the initiate in the manner of a woman (Eliade 1960).

Engulfment myths are many. We find them in the most diverse cultures—in Africa, Oceania, Lapland, Finland, among the Eskimos—and they involve men, women, and children (Eliade 1960; Campbell 1949).

The engulfment by the monster "signifies the re-entry into a pre-formed, embryonic state of being," the "return to the germinal mode of being," which implies death as well, since one must die to one's existence in order to return to the "beginning" (Eliade 1960, 223).

Thus Marjorie's journey into the entrails of the whale may bear the meaning of a symbolic death. Frances G. Wickes (1978) notes that rebirth and death are present in the lives of small children as well as adults: "Progress and regression, rebirth and death are present from the earliest days, and are shown in the little acts of the little child as well as in the larger acts of the larger adult" (57).

The whale entrails where Marjorie implants herself are dark green. Her drawing shows her, head down, surrounded by tissues that follow the contours of her body. The forest green that she uses in her drawing represents the insides of the body of the whale as a kind of fertile terrain, suggesting that Marjorie takes root in a verdant place where she can flourish. The therapeutic qualities that the color green carries include the return of life in spring, balance, health, renewal, and the abundance of life, and this green links the interior of the belly of the whale to a nurturant and regenerating environment.

As a place of death, the belly of the whale also contains the promise of new life. Jung (1956) conceives the psychic phenomenon of engulfment by the monster as a regression of libido into deeper layers of existence, into the intrauterine life, at a stage that goes beyond the personal psyche, with the libido erupting into the collective psyche. Jung observes that the regressive libido may become fixated in a primitive state, but that it can also work free from the maternal hold and bring the possibility of new life back to the surface.[1]

The whale engulfs at the same time that it delivers from the water. This is why the whale has been compared to Noah's Ark over the waters of the

Flood (Chevalier and Gheerbrant 1973). Drowned and subjected to the immensity of the ocean, Marjorie is saved by the sea monster from within which she now sails.

Marjorie is by herself in her adventure with the sea monster. There are no references to other people in the dream. The encounter with the monster is a face-to-face meeting with oneself, observes Claudette Oriol-Boyer (1975). That between Marjorie and the whale is one of the most intimate forms of contact. Marjorie and the mammal are almost at one. Marjorie is contained inside the mammal, which surrounds and envelops her like an embrace.

The strategies described so far have been active strategies: to kill the monster, to transform it, to stroke it, to flee it. But the strategy implicit in the present situation consists, on the contrary, in ceasing all action and in becoming, by oneself, an object of transformation. This is the meaning of the symbolic death that precedes any new beginning.

Engulfed in the whale, Marjorie must give up control. She must go where the sea monster goes. The confinement that being engulfed results in leads to attitudes of expectancy and openness to the unpredictable, as well as to a kind of surrender. These attitudes contain subtle forms of activity that substitute for outer activity and counterbalance it when outer activity becomes impossible.

Dream Four

> Marjorie dreams that she is able to ride a two-wheeled bicycle, which in waking reality she cannot do. In her dream, it is her birthday and she receives a bicycle as a gift from her father and mother.

Amplification

Dream Four breaks away from the deep level of Dream Three and takes us into the world of Marjorie's everyday life. In addition to expressing Marjorie's desire for a bicycle for her birthday, this dream shows her in complete mastery of her vehicle, reflecting a new competence.

From one dream to the next, the various vehicles recur. The baby carriage, the train, the car, and the bicycle express in many ways, over and over again, the experience of movement and displacement in Marjorie's psychic life.

Dream Five

> Marjorie goes to a mountain and sees a small baby. She takes it and later drops it. Then she sees a cross and climbs onto it. "I was doing like Jesus," she specifies after drawing the dream.

The drawing shows Marjorie's silhouette (in black) climbing the mountain (yellow). On top of the mountain, we see Marjorie holding the baby (both are orange), the dropped child (in black), and the cross with Marjorie upon it (both are orange).

Amplification

The meaning of Marjorie's odyssey reveals itself from one dream to the next. Her journey, which began in the familiar setting of a stroll in a baby carriage pushed by a friend, now more and more resembles the stages of a heroic quest. These stages include departure for the adventure, passage through the belly of the whale, and now ascent up the mountain and climbing onto the cross, with all the initiation-related meanings attached to them. These stages of the heroic journey have been identified by Joseph Campbell (1949) in *The Hero with a Thousand Faces*.

Marjorie has left the baby carriage and car, and it is on foot that she encounters the present stage of her journey. She walks on the earth, she climbs the mountain. After the ocean drowns, dissolves, and absorbs her into its depths, she arrives on the firm and secure earth, which supports and calls for the effort of ascending. The movement of descending to the root of life is reversed by this movement of ascending to the summit of the mountain. The symbolic death in the sunken hollow of the belly of the whale finds its echo in the symbolic death on the cross (see fig. 14).

The symbolism of ascension may involve climbing mountains or stairs or flying into the atmosphere, and it may manifest itself in dreams, active imagination, mythological or folkloric stories, or ecstatic experience. But it "always refers to a breaking-out from a situation that has become 'blocked' or 'petrified'; a rupture of the plane which makes it possible to pass from one mode of being into another—in short, liberty 'of movement,' freedom to change the situation, to abolish a conditioning system" (Eliade 1960, 118). Mircea Eliade notes that the type of "waking dream" that Robert Desoille asked his patients to imagine most frequently, in order to bring about their psychological healing, was precisely climbing a stairway or ascending a mountain.

After the return to early childhood, the dissolution in the primal ocean, and the descent to the belly of the whale, Marjorie becomes engaged in an opposite psychic movement of climbing toward the summit of the mountain. The summit represents the highest point. It is an arrival point, like the belly of the whale. Marjorie's walk up the mountain is not errant wandering, it is directed toward a summit surmounted by the cross.

On the mountain, Marjorie sees a baby. It is there, all by itself, calling on Marjorie to react. Marjorie takes the baby. Her drawing shows her holding the baby, with the baby and Marjorie forming a single configuration in orange, as if both partook of the same essence. This maternal Marjorie is in the posi-

Figure 14. Drawing 18" x 12". The ascent of the mountain. From left to right: Marjorie climbing, Marjorie holding the child, the dropped child, Marjorie on the cross.

tion of mother toward child, although she occupied the position of baby in the first dream. This role reversal for Marjorie coincides with the reversal of her psychic movement from descent to ascension.

The child, picked up, is dropped. From being orange along with Marjorie in the drawing, it becomes black. The dropped child evokes a loss. The dream suggests that Marjorie drops her early childhood, that she loses the baby toward which she was regressing in the initial dream of the baby carriage. The dropping of the baby appears to be the end of a regressive process begun at the very beginning of the series, the regression into early childhood with the dream of the baby carriage and into prenatal life with the dream of the whale. In the present dream, Marjorie is not identified with the child or the fetus; she is the mother who takes the child, then is separated from it by dropping it. The child falls. The dropping comes as something unexpected, quickly and decisively.

After dropping the baby, Marjorie climbs onto the cross, identifying herself with an adult spiritual hero. Jung (1956) sees in the symbol of the sacrificed god that is at the heart of many religions, some of them pre-Christian, the expression of a significant transformation. He conceives the sacrifice of the hero as a renunciation of the return to the maternal womb for the benefit of acquiring immortality. In this sense, this sacrifice is the opposite of regression: "The sacrifice is the very reverse of regression—it is a successful canalization of libido into the symbolic equivalent of the mother, and hence a spiritualization of it" (263).

Marie-Louise von Franz (1974) interprets the symbol of the crucifixion as the expression of a conflict between the unconscious, with its ineluctable process of psychic growth, and the will of the conscious personality:

> Part of our life passes like a drama written by a novelist biographer, but behind that there is a mysterious process of growth which follows its own laws and takes place behind the biographical peripetias of life and goes from childhood to old age. In a mythological connection, the greater human being, the anthropos, is likened to a tree. The human being is suspended on the tree because the conscious human constantly pulls away, trying to free himself and to act freely and consciously and he is then painfully pulled back to the inner process. The struggle reveals a tragic constellation if it is represented in this painful form. That is why the whole philosophy of the Christian religion has a tragic view of life: to follow Christ we have to accept mortification and repress certain natural growth. The basic idea is that human life is based on conflict and strives toward spiritualization which does not come of itself but is brought forth with pain. . . .
>
> Whenever the conscious and animal personality is in conflict with the inner process of growth, it suffers crucifixion; it is in the situation of the God suspended on the tree and is involuntarily nailed to an unconscious development from which it would like to break away but cannot. We know the states one falls into when nailed down to something greater than ourselves which does not allow us to move and which outgrows us. (39)

Von Franz speaks of how the "mysterious process of growth which follows its own laws" behind the outer events—the peripetias—of our lives goes on from childhood to adulthood. Adults tend to forget that the conflict between these two dimensions of life can occur in childhood as well as in adulthood. When this conflict between the inner growth process and the conscious personality is represented in the painful form of being hung or crucified, it can mean that the conflict has reached its acute phase. In light of von Franz's remarks, Marjorie's climbing onto the cross points to an inner conflict and to the pain that such a conflict entails.

However, the cross is also a sign of unification. It symbolizes the reconciliation of opposites, its two axes penetrating each other and meeting in the center. The cross can express the transcendence of a situation in which the being is divided in herself or himself, torn into opposing and contradictory polarities. From the beginning of her dream odyssey, Marjorie is subjected to opposing and contradictory movements that pull her forward and backward, downward and upward. By baby carriage, by car, on foot, we have seen her go first toward an unknown destination, then toward the ocean and the mountain, while at the same time she has been going more deeply into the far-reaching past of early childhood and prenatal life. We have seen her ascend to the summit of the mountain after having descended to the roots of life through regression and symbolic death. This movement itself expresses the four directions of the cross.

The top of the mountain with its cross is a symbol of the "center of the world" and of the "axis of the world" (Eliade 1963). The line Marjorie's inner voyage travels takes her from the center, which the baby carriage represented, to a movement of descent to the belly of the whale, and up again to the transcendent center of the summit of the mountain. Marjorie's itinerary follows the vital current that passes through the center, a center recurring in several guises.

As a place of death, the belly of the whale contained a promise of renewal; as a place of sacrifice, the cross also bears a creative potential. In his reflection on creation myths that include the sacrifice of a divinity, Eliade speaks of the fundamental idea of these practices, that life can be born only through the sacrifice of another life: "The fundamental idea is that Life can only take birth from another life which is sacrificed. The violent death is creative—in this sense, that the life which is sacrificed manifests itself in a more brilliant form upon another plane of existence" (1960, 184).

Marjorie's walk to the summit of the mountain is an autonomous act that she accomplishes on her own. And her climb onto the cross remains, in Campbell's words, "to the eye and heart a silent sign," a gesture that preserves its full mystery (1964, 334).

Dream Six

> There is a storm and it brings the rain. There is a little girl. She returns to her house because of the rain. When the storm ends, Marjorie goes out. She sees another little girl. They hear the Fire Department truck. They see a house that burns. Then they see the Fire Department people arrive and stop the fire.

Amplification

The dream of the storm takes us back to the familiar surrounding of Marjorie's house. The movement that has carried Marjorie in the baby carriage to the ocean and the mountain has stopped. The dynamic focus of the present dream is on a storm that leads to a house on fire.

A storm is a powerful and violent discharge, an accumulation of energy suddenly released in the form of rain that makes everything fertile. The storm that precedes the rain is an epiphany of the life force. The sky, which the Greeks personified as Ouranos, the male-who-is-fruitful (Eliade, 1963), is a sky with the kind of fecundity that comes from the water and fire of the storm.

But in this dream, the storm brings on the rain and is at the origin of the house fire. Marjorie comes out of her house after the storm and with the other girl discovers that a house is burning. The lightning bolt both engenders and destroys at the same time (Chevalier and Gheerbrant 1973). Marjorie enters into contact with the power of nature in its destructive form as well. The process of the house's destruction is finally controlled by the intervention of the people from the Fire Department, who represent an exterior and institutional force, like the ambulance team in the dream of the train accident.

The meaning of the burning house remains incomplete without information about Marjorie's personal and family life. Even if the house is a symbol of personal identity, it is also the family center, and as such its meaning here escapes us. The return to the domestic environment brings with it other people, such as the little girl and the people from the Fire Department, and breaks away from the deeply solitary character of Dreams Three and Five. Finally, this dream introduces the elements of air and fire, which come after the elements of water and earth in the dreams of the ocean and the mountain.

Dream Seven

> Marjorie has a dog that bites her. She goes home and puts on a Band-Aid. The dog leaves. It digs and finds a bone, digs the bone up, and goes. Marjorie comes out again.

Amplification

After the violence of nature comes the violence of the domestic animal. The dog that bites Marjorie is her own dog. It is again difficult to know what Marjorie's relation to the animal is, and what the meaning of this interaction is, without information on the subjective and personal meaning that the animal has for her.

After the aggression from the dog, Marjorie withdraws to devote her attention to the care of her wound. Her creative energy is not invested in fighting with the animal but in the treatment of the wound that the dog inflicts. Instead of doing something to the dog, Marjorie does something for herself: she works on her healing.

The dog digs and finds a bone, takes it out, and goes. If we look closely at the drawing of the bone in the hole, we can see the similarity between

the shape of the bone contained in the hole, which is represented by a circular scribble, and the green entrails of the whale that surround Marjorie at
the bottom of the ocean in the previous drawing. The bone in the hole is
an image with ingredients similar to that of Marjorie in the belly of the whale
at the bottom of the ocean. We may wonder if the bone in the hole is not
an expression of symbolic burial, with the purpose of healing, fortifying, or
satisfying an initiatory rite. Such symbolic rituals always symbolize regeneration by contact with the forces of the earth.

Dream Eight

Marjorie and the members of her family are at their cottage. Next door there is
a man whom they know. He has decided to destroy the cottage of Marjorie's family,
saying that Marjorie's whole family was going to live in his house. He has a big machine
with "a pointed thing" and the machine has begun to destroy the porch.

Amplification

The dream of the neighbor reveals a third form of violence that Marjorie con-
tacts. This is human violence in its male form, expressed here in the symbol of
the machine. The male figures seen so far in Marjorie's dream series include the
men on the ambulance team and those of the Fire Department, as well as Marjorie's father (with her mother), from whom she receives a bicycle as a birthday
present. There is also a reference to Jesus in the dream of the cross. And in Dream
Eight, the male figure takes the form of the neighbor and appears in an aggressive
and destructive form.

The development of the relationship to males and the masculine constitutes
as aspect of a female's psychic development that would require a study of its own.
Here the limitations of our study permit us to say only that the encounter with
the figure of the male adult is part of Marjorie's odyssey, the odyssey of a five-year-
old girl in whom consciousness awakens and differentiates.

Dream Nine

One time it was dark. It was night. Marjorie had taken a flashlight. Then afterward, she went to her house.
In the drawing, Marjorie is behind a screen of black, scribbling with an enormous
flashlight.

Amplification

Again the horizontal movement returns, a movement that has taken Marjorie
from the domestic environment to the ocean and the mountain. Here the horizon-

tal movement does not lead her away but rather takes her back home. In the
night, equipped with a lamp, Marjorie is making her way home.

Night corresponds to the darkness, and penetrating the darkness corresponds
to descending into the underworld. Night also symbolizes a time for gesta-
tion and germination, a time when the future grows and is fashioned, and
when the return to light is prepared. In descending into the belly of the whale,
Marjorie entered into the night. Now we see her walking through the night
with a light, and equipped with this lamp she crosses the night without being
ambushed as she makes her way home. The dream of the lamp in the night
suggests the way of return and Marjorie's return from the night.

Dream Ten

Marjorie is on the seashore and she wants to try to swim. She goes into the
deep and drowns. Then she comes up again. Someone comes and picks her
up. She later says that this person "saves" her. She draws a sun "because it was
beautiful."

Amplification

This dream brings Marjorie to the water for a second time. Finding herself
on the seashore, she ventures into the water, drawn by the desire to try to
swim. The water is shown as a long and narrow band that crosses the width
of the drawing paper. In the drawing of the whale dream, the water was shown
as a large rectangle. The water of this dream and the water of the whale dream
appear to have different natures. One resembles a stream or a river, since it
is horizontal, and the other resembles a deep and circumscribed mass of water
such as a lake, sea, or ocean.

Marjorie wants "to try to swim." After having moved in many ways—on
the firm earth, by baby carriage, by car, on a bicycle, and on foot—she now
wants to try the fluid element. Marjorie is looking for a new mastery. To swim
implies moving into water by propelling oneself with one's arms and legs
turning as if they were fins and tentacles. Swimmers thrust through water
by propelling themselves to assist in movement. They swim not only in the
water but *with* the water. Thus there is a dynamic play established between
swimmer and water, water and swimmer, creating the movement of swimming.

In the dream of the whale, the plunge into the ocean seemed to signify ego
dissolution and the return to an undifferentiated consciousness at the origins
of life. Here Marjorie moves into the water not to dissolve but, on the contrary, with the intention of staying in contact with her own power and her
capacity to do so.

But for the second time Marjorie drowns. The drowning marks a turning point, a moment of passage from one state of consciousness to another. It also implies a new descent toward the depths. For the second time Marjorie sinks toward the bottom. Then suddenly this descent stops and she begins to ascend again, coming to the surface, where someone saves her.

Marjorie's emergence from the water appears as a sign of rebirth. After the passage through the belly of the whale and the experience of the cross, Marjorie resurfaces. The drawing shows her emerging from the water, while on the shore there is a character illustrated with many colors (arms and head in yellow, body in red, legs in blue). This dream character who "saves" her seems to be an unknown and numinous being, judging from Marjorie's drawing. This male figure embodies a benevolent force. The magnificence of the moment was summarized by Marjorie when she said that she has put the sun in the drawing "because it was beautiful" (see fig. 15—though the sun is not visible).

Immersion in water followed by surfacing is also a general form of baptism. For a long time baptism was practiced by total immersion, and even today, regardless of the various modifications introduced into the liturgy by different Christian traditions, the baptismal ritual continues to consist in two gestures and phases of symbolic meaning—immersion, which in most traditions is now reduced to aspersion, and surfacing or emergence—which symbolize purification and regeneration. Commenting on the symbolism of immersion, Eliade says: "In water everything is 'dissolved,' every 'form' is broken up, everything that has happened ceases to exist; nothing that was before remains after immersion in water, not an outline, not a 'sign,' not an 'event.'. . . Breaking up all forms, doing away with all the past, water possesses this power of purifying, of regenerating, of giving new birth; for what is immersed in it 'dies,' and, rising again from the water, is like a child without any sin or any past, able to receive a new revelation and begin a new and *real* life" (1963, 194). Eliade's interpretation illumines the sense of renewal present in Dream Ten.

Dream Eleven

Marjorie goes to the store and the "mister" there is a monster. She says, "I would like an apple." He gives it to her and she goes home.

Amplification

In the first dream of the series, Marjorie found herself face to face with the monster represented as an animal and she awoke as a means of escaping it. Dream Eleven again puts her in front of the monster, who this time is in human

Figure 15. Drawing 24" x 18". The emergence. Marjorie's "savior," on the left, and Marjorie emerging from the water.

form. As a male adult, the monster-storekeeper is also linked to the "man with the machine" who attacked the cottage of Marjorie's family in a previous dream.

Marjorie's odyssey follows an itinerary that starting from the monster and going through water, reaches the summit of the mountain, goes through water again, and returns to the monster. But between the beginning and the end of this series, there is a deep change. When Marjorie returns to the water for a second time, instead of staying at the bottom she comes up to the surface. Similarly, in Dream Eleven, when she stands in front of the monster, her attitude is changed. Instead of waking up in order to escape the monster in her dream, her strategy consists in resorting to the spoken word to obtain what she wants, after which she leaves.

In fairy tales and myths, the hero or heroine is on a search for a treasure that the dragon possesses. He or she must approach the monster and obtain the treasure without falling victim to the danger that the monster represents. In *Wassilissa*, a fairy tale analyzed by von Franz (1976), Wassilissa lives with her stepmother, her two adoptive sisters, and her father. One day when the father is absent, the two sisters, jealous of Wassilissa, send her to get fire at Baba Yaga's house in the forest. Baba Yaga has a reputation for eating all those who approach her abode. Wassilissa makes her way to the witch's house, and there Baba Yaga keeps her a prisoner. Each day, Wassilissa must do more and more chores: sweep the floor, wash the laundry, set the table, sort varieties of seeds.

Wassilissa is accompanied on her quest by a magic doll, a gift from her deceased mother, and this doll assists her in her chores, allowing her to meet Baba Yaga's demands and avoid being eaten. One day while Baba Yaga is eating, Wassilissa inquires if she may ask her a few questions. "Ask," says Baba Yaga, "but remember that not all questions are wise; much knowledge makes one old" (145). Wassilissa asks a question concerning a knight whom she had seen pass by during her arrival at the witch's house. But she stops asking questions at that point and refrains from asking about the three pairs of hands that she has seen grinding the witch's grain. Her wise attitude earns her the respect of Baba Yaga, who thereupon frees her and gives her the fire that she has come for.

Just as Wassilissa knew how to ask the right questions, Marjorie seems to have the right attitude and to say the words necessary to obtain what she needs from the monster. Marjorie wants an apple—a fruit, a food, that stands for unity and knowledge, and for renewal and perpetual freshness.

Marjorie's transaction with the monster, during which she avoids the danger that he represents, shows a dynamic interplay between them, one that goes beyond a relationship of domination and submission. Marjorie does not subdue the monster, nor does she vanquish or destroy it. She annuls the malefic power of the monster and remains intact.

Marjorie comes toward the monster without weapons but with the power only of her spoken word. Her spoken word is measured and spare, and it comes like a ripened fruit after the long silence that has until now marked her dreams.

Chapter Eight

The Monster as Initiator

Seen from the perspective of the monster theme, the oneiric adventure of the child on the threshold of "the age of reason," around age seven, resembles a heroic quest. Like the hero of fairy tales and myths, the child in his or her dreams goes to the forest, the mountain, or the ocean and there encounters the monster; or the child is called to an adventure by the monster who breaks into the intimacy of the family dwelling. The child's first impulse is often to retreat. In his or her dreams the child escapes, calls for help, and falls into unconsciousness by sinking into sleep or going numb or blind. But then the child takes up the challenge raised by the monster and moves forward into the adventure, alone or with the help of an ally. In the three series studied, we have seen the child come to victory in combat with the enemy, persevere until a monster is tamed, and surrender to the transformative power of the monster and be regenerated by it.

The call to adventure, the refusal to heed that call, the engagement in adventure, the combat with the monster, the taming of the monster, and the engulfment by the monster all constitute stages of the hero's odyssey. The hero's victory over the monster—whether it takes the form of putting the monster to death, taming it, or being engulfed by it followed by rebirth—always bears the character of initiation. The child's victory over the monster of her or his nights, when it is the result of a genuine intrapsychic process, also contains a potential for initiating that child.

The Mystery of the Monster

The monster is linked with the deep forces that govern the evolution of human life: the sacred, Eros, death, rebirth. Each of the dream series studied illumines a particular face of the monster. Eric's series presents the monster as a numinous and terrible power. Pierre's series reveals the monster as a being who metamorphoses. Marjorie's series features a monster who is a container for death and a passage to renewed life. As a numinous and terrible power, the monster evokes the sense of the sacred, known as *tremendum*; as a being of metamorphosis, the monster suggests the realm of Eros; as a container of death and the passage to new life, the monster is linked with the mysteries of death and rebirth.

The Monster and the Tremendum

Eric's series shows the monster to be a power both incommensurable and "terrible." We recall the monster of Eric's initial dream, "a huge enormous beast. . .as tall as the sky," which brought on the collapse of the earth, its engulfment by the waters, and which shook the foundations of the child's universe. The monster that unleashed these apocalyptic consequences appeared as a terrible being with powers transcending human limitations.

The terrible aspect of the monster that awakens disquiet and fear in the soul is the aspect most commonly spoken of when children tell their dreams and fantasies. The word *terrible* is rich with nuances. On the one hand, the word refers to that which induces an intense terror and is thus synonymous with "scary" or "frightening." On the other hand, the word suggests something that exceeds the boundaries of the ordinary, and in this sense it has the connotations of "remarkable," "extraordinary," or even "formidable."

In Latin, the word *tremendum* (terrible) comes from the noun *tremor*, which means "a trembling," "a quivering." Thus as *tremendum* the monster is the one that makes us shudder, that unsettles, that shakes and paralyzes us with fear. But the monster is also the one that moves us, and we cannot fully understand its nature and the fascination it exerts without speaking of the numinous reality of which it partakes.

In *The Idea of the Holy*, Rudolph Otto (1958) describes the sacred as *mysterium tremendum*. The expression refers to the mystery in the face of which a person is overcome by an emotion likened to fear mixed with respect. According to Otto, the sense of awe and religious dread that accompanies the experience of *mysterium tremendum*, even in its most elevated forms, has its roots in previous historical stages of primitive "daemonic dread,"[1] beginning with the uncanny feeling felt toward what seems eerie or weird. It is this sacred fear, this primary and unique feeling deriving from nothing else, that is for Otto at the origin of the entire religious development of history.[2]

This uncanny feeling is sometimes sensed in the tone of the child's telling of the dream experience. In the presentation of his initial dream, for example, Eric introduces us to a situation filled with a strange mystery. Eric is in bed when suddenly he finds himself caught in entangling ropes around his bed.

Then there appears the fabulous monster, and a voice comes as if from somewhere else, announcing the collapse of the earth. Pierre's adventure also begins under the sign of the unfamiliar. Pierre hears a singular sound and he tries to find its origin. He explores the house from top to bottom and discovers a "strange bug" downstairs. He goes upstairs again, looks out his window, and there witnesses the arrival of a flying saucer. This tone of the uncanny is also present in Michel's encounter with the dragon who spat fire and in Mireille's dream of the house and the giant flower.

Yet even in the dream of a young child, the *tremendum* may acquire the most extreme character, as well as the subtlest nuance. With Eric, it takes terrifying form as an angry demon; with Marjorie, it has the resonance of the ocean depths to which the whale carries her; in Pierre's act of taming, it has the subtlety of a moment of grace when destiny is reversed.

The monster participates in *mysterium tremendum*. In her commentary on the monster of a Chinese tale, von Franz (1974) notes that the monster is experienced as something supernatural, thus accounting for the complexity of the emotion it inspires: "If we take the monster of this story as a personification of such a phenomenon of evil nature, then we can say that it is super-natural. It is highly numinous and therefore highly fascinating, which is why one has all this pleasurable excitement about it. And it is frightening! It is as terrifying as it is attractive, and it is a non-personal and non-human phenomenon" (125).

The monster fascinates the child and gives him the chills at the same time. We have only to think of the excitement children feel when they play wolf: "Let's go into the woods while the wolf isn't there. Wolf, are you there? Do you hear? Big, humped, pointy nose!" The wolf answers, "The wolf puts his boots on," and the other children scream and shiver. "The wolf puts his coat on." More screaming and shivering, until the wolf puts on "his hat"[3] and comes out to catch a child who will take the part of the wolf. We can also think of the excitement with which children tirelessly experience again and again Little Red Riding Hood and the wolf, Goldilocks and the Three Bears, and so on.

In puberty rites as practiced in traditional societies, the first and most terrible initiation is that of the sacred as *tremendum* (Eliade 1958). We may imagine the novices, separated from their mothers, taken far away from familiar places by unknown masked men, while in the forest the terrifying sounds of the bull-roarers resonate. These sounds, which are likened to the releasing of primordial forces, incarnate the voice of the initiating gods.

The bull-roarer, or rhomb, is a piece of wood about nine inches long and two inches wide, at one end of which there is a hole for a string. By rotating the bull-roarer one produces a sound like that of thunder or a bellowing bull. During the night, the mysterious bellowing comes from the forest and fills the initiates with a sacred terror, since it announces the approach of the divinity.

As a numinous and powerful force, the monster resembles the impressive divinity announced by the bull-roarers, and the terror inspired by the encounter with the monster recalls the sacred terror of novices hearing the sounds of the bull-roarers as they presage the presence of the initiating god.

The Austrian poet Rainer Maria Rilke has suggested that fear is our own strength still too large for us. The terror brought on by Eric's apocalyptic monster is as real as the imminence of his struggle in assuring his psychological integrity. Marjorie's stupor is vivid to us, in the face of the animal monster of her initial dream, as is the emotion of Pierre, who attempts to escape from the woman with the mirror. The fear of the dark, the fear of the night, the fear of the phantasmagorical, animal, or human monster that appears in dreams, strikes children dumb and contracts them, but also mobilizes them. Fear has its unexplainable features, as does the monster, but we may observe fear's movements and vibrations, pay attention to what it signals, feel its vitality, and learn to use it in a creative way.

In the *I Ching*, the Chinese Book of Changes, the hexagram *Tchen* means "the arousing or the shock" and has as its image the thunder bursting forth from the earth, the shock of which causes fear and trembling. "When a man has learned within his heart what fear and trembling mean," says the commentary, "he is safeguarded against any terror produced by outside influences" (198). The perspective of the *I Ching* makes room for knowledge and progress. And there is reason to believe that the first confrontations with fear in meeting the dream characters of childhood constitute the first steps toward the acquisition of a knowing that leads to wisdom.

As *tremendum*, the monster is the awakener. The advent of the beast unleashes Eric's movement, the animal monster alerts Marjorie, the strange "bug" intrigues Pierre. The monster is action, an active energy that obliges and engages anyone on whose road it presents itself, and does this whatever the age of the person.

The Monster and Eros

Pierre's active, curious, and creative approach to the monster through his dreams leads to a series of partial transformations of the monster. The most complete transformation, however, happens as Pierre approaches the crocodile with a movement of the heart when he tames it. Transforming the crocodile into a small soft animal under Pierre's caressing stroke is a motif that pertains to the domain of Eros.

Freud's psychoanalytic theory has habituated us to associate Eros with only the sexual and to reduce Eros to it. But Eros extends beyond the sexual, and the sexual is only one of the many forms that expresses Eros. Among the ancient Greeks, the god Eros was linked with the originating principle of all manifestations. Born from the Egg of winged Night's depths and the rushing Wind, the god Eros was brought forth in matriarchal Greece as a cosmogonic principle, making creation and union possible in all its forms. Only later was Eros conceived first as the companion and then as the son of Aphrodite. This text from an ancient Greek author describes how the god of love came into the world:

> Night was a bird with black wings. Ancient Night conceived of the Wind and laid her silver Egg in the gigantic lap of Darkness. From the Egg sprang the son of the rushing Wind, a God with golden wings. He is called Eros, the God of love, but this is only one name, the loveliest of all names this god bore.
>
> The god's other names, such of them as we still know, sound very scholastic, but even they refer only to particular details of the old story. His name of Pro-togonos means only that he was the "firstborn" of all gods. His name of Phanes exactly explains what he did when he was hatched from the Egg: he revealed and brought into light everything that had previously lain hidden in the silver Egg—in other words, the whole world. (Neumann 1973, 53).

The unifying and creative function that Eros represents governs life from birth until death. The beginnings of the life of a child are characterized by a relationship to the mother and to the world that Neumann, following Lucien Lévy-Bruhl, has described as "participation mystique." Since the dualities distinguishing ego from mother and ego from world have not yet been constellated in the child's psyche, the child's reality includes the mother's reality, life, and the world in one unity: "In the post-uterine phase of existence in unitary reality," says Neumann, "the child lives in a total *participation mystique*, a psychic mother-fluid in which everything is still in suspension and from which the opposites, ego and Self, subject and object, individual and world have yet to be crystallized. That is why this phase is associated with 'oceanic feeling' which repeatedly makes its appearance even in adults when unitary reality complements, breaks through, or replaces everyday conscious reality with its polarisation into subject and object" (1973, 15).

The Oedipal relationship takes root in Eros. The Oedipal quest is fundamentally a quest for love and recognition; it is grounded in the girl's primordial need to be loved and recognized by her father, and the son's need to be loved by his mother, loved for themselves as unique and distinct beings on the path of their destiny. The creative and instinctual movement that propels children toward life; toward the development of their physical, emotional, and imaginative resources; toward the knowing and the exploration of their surrounding universe—this movement is also a manifestation of the vital energy that Eros governs. As the power of origins, Eros presides over the first periods of existence of the baby; and he is on the path of the child who, by means of magical thinking, apprehends reality for its symbolic, sense-connected, and relational properties; Eros is on the path of the adolescent who brings love to birth, and on the path of the awakening adult whose consciousness may have the capacity to perceive the living link uniting all that there is.

But the mystery of the god Eros is deep, and contact with it throughout life is always paradoxical. This is also true of its manifestation in the life of the child. Thus the child's quest for love and recognition in relation to the parent of the opposite sex also bears frustration, pain, resentment, power struggles with the rival parent, competition, and fratricidal jealousies. And the desire that propels the child toward new physical, cognitive, and imaginative frontiers also engenders fear of the unknown, guilt experienced for one's actions, and anxiety in the face of limitations on one's resources and possibilities.

The monster of metamorphosis incarnates this intimate marriage between creative forces of life and their opposites. Vital energy evolves, is converted, and is transformed through a dynamic movement between opposing polarities. Growth occurs not in a one-sided way but by involving all dimensions of human experience and the child's experience.

The complexity of the mystery of Eros is reflected in how the god is sometimes conceived as a god-demon. In *Septem Sermones ad Mortuous*, Jung, using the voice of Basilides, a Gnostic author of the second century A.D., wrote of two god-demons, one Eros and the other the Tree of Life:

> The god-sun is the highest good; the devil is the opposite. Thus have ye two gods. But there are many high and good things and many great evils. Among these are two god-devils; the one is the BURNING ONE, the other the GROW-ING ONE.
> The burning one is EROS, who hath the form of flame. Flame giveth light because it consumeth. The growing one is the TREE OF LIFE. It buddeth, as in growing it heapeth up living stuff. (1967, 23)

In the myth of Eros and Psyche, the god-demon duality is again expressed. As the oracle announces that a demon will come to take possession of Psyche, who is adorned for her impending wedding, it is Eros (Cupid, in Latin) who declares himself her spouse. Later, Psyche's jealous sisters liken Eros to a dragon capable of devouring Psyche and her child. Revealed under Psyche's lamp, Eros shows himself to be none other than a god. Likened here to a demon, there to a dragon, the god of love is a being of metamorphosis.

In fairy tales and legends, the motif of the monster transformed, through the influence of the openness of the heroine's or hero's heart, into a princess or prince charming is a motif also under the sign of Eros. With Pierre it is the innocence of the heart of a child that prompts the metamorphosis of the crocodile into a small and gentle animal, but this metamorphosis also partakes of the mystery of the god-demon.

The Monster, Death, and Rebirth

In Marjorie's series, the monster reveals itself as the one who simultaneously devours and despoils, the one who takes life into itself and gives it back changed. We recall the journey taking Marjorie into the depth of the sea monster's belly and beyond, to her reemergence. The engulfing monster symbolizes the forces of absorption and perpetual regeneration of life, and it is linked with the mysteries of death and rebirth.

The theme of the engulfing monster frequently arises in the dreams and fantasies of children. The beast in Eric's dream takes him into his jaws, then throws him into the water. Pierre comes to grips with the Blob, which threatens to devour everybody if it is not kept in the freezer. The wolf swallows the mannequin that stands for Odile's double. The whale eats Marjorie.

The mystery of the return to origins suggested by the engulfment theme repeats itself for children and adults and is found in contemporary adult life as well as in ancient myths. Marjorie's voyage into the belly of the sea monster followed by her reemergence finds its echo in the odyssey described in Julie Stanton's poem *La nomade* (1983). An anonymous, journeying Everywoman, the heroine of Stanton's poem, gradually surrenders her eyes, her head of hair, her face, and her beauty to return to the belly of the Beast, an animal with golden nostrils, from which she will reemerge with renewed strength:

> The bray of the Beast opens its chest up
> passageway greatly allowing
> exiting already
> She has recognized the surroundings
> "the deep enchantment"
> where one becomes prisoner without dying
> and supreme under the day's wound
> the throatcanyon of time
> sun deep in the cloister....
>
> And so She is in the Beast
> her life suspended and yet she has life
> passenger on a boat henceforth dockable
> henceforth this place the acquiescing
> silky slide of mucous membranes. (42–45)[4]

The descent of Marjorie into the belly of the whale, her suspension on the cross, and her emergence from the waters with help from the unknown savior also evoke the perennial trajectory of Psyche, Persephone, and Inanna into and through the underworld. In the Sumerian myth of Inanna (Perera, 1981) the goddess of heaven and earth decides to descend into the underworld, where Ereshkigal reigns. Ereshkigal suspends Inanna's corpse on a peg like rotting meat. It is Enki, the god of waters and wisdom, who comes to rescue Inanna. He creates two mourners from the dirt under his fingernails, and they slip unnoticed into the underworld to bring Inanna food and the water of life.

Marjorie returns into the belly of the whale. The Nomad enters into the chest cavity of the Beast of golden nostrils. Inanna descends into the great nether regions. The Nomad gradually loses her eyes, her head of hair, her beauty. Inanna gives up her adornments and articles of clothes, one after the other. Marjorie drops the baby. The peg on which the goddess suspends Inanna's corpse recalls the cross on which Marjorie climbs. And in the same way that Inanna is saved by the intervention of Enki, the god of waters and wisdom, Marjorie is pulled out of the waters by the unknown dream character. Finally, the resurging waters from which Marjorie returns are like the water of life, which restores Inanna.

The belly of the whale, the cavity of the Beast with the golden nostrils, the belly of the earth, the peg for the goddess and the cross, the unknown savior and the god Enki, the resurging waters and the water of life—all constitute symbolic forms in resonance with one another. The level of consciousness engaged in the experience of the descent into the belly of the monster followed by a reemergence could not be the same at age five and in adulthood, but the dreams attest that the child participates in the initiatory movement of deaths and rebirths that govern the evolution of human life.

Children's Tasks for Growing Up

Each approach to the encounter with the monster also illustrates a task on the road toward awakening the child's consciousness: combat with the monster suggests the child's mastery of his or her own strength, taming of the monster points toward openness and the child's developing relational capacity, and engulfment by the monster refers to surrendering to or participating in the life forces that can also regenerate. The first is linked with power, the second pertains to the domain of the heart, and the third concerns the capacity to be.

Transitions in the Lives of Five-Year-Olds

On the threshold of later childhood leading to the age of reason, the child faces a new set of situations. At that age, the child emerges from early childhood, the family, and preschool and prepares to enter school. From then on, the family circle opens up to a larger circle encompassing the community of peers and other adults, including parental substitutes, schoolteachers, and sports instructors. To the creative and free play of the child are added the art of doing, the notion of work, and the sense of competence (Erickson 1959, 1963).

Five years old is also the age for resolution of what Freud called "the Oedipal complex," in which the girl's wish for exclusive attachment to the father and the son's wish for exclusive attachment to the mother are resolved by the realization of the limits that the parental couple implies, of social taboos in force, and by the identification with the parent of one's own sex. Finally, this age marks the exit from the Garden of Eden, the loss of the original unity, the entry into the world of guilt and of good and evil. On the threshold of the age of reason, children encounter the phenomenon of the shadow as their dreams portray it, and begin to be aware of the negative side of their actions.

In the area of dream life, the amplitude of dreams increases starting from age four or five, and the structure of the dreams changes (Foulkes 1982). Furthermore, the symbolic content of dreams becomes richer and more complex (Freud 1915). There is the appearance of the first archetypal dreams (Jung 1956), an increase in dreams depicting the monster (Elkan 1969), and an increase in nightmares (Ames 1964).

A new energy becomes available that will favor the child's growth on all levels—physical, emotional, and mental. On the cognitive level, as Piaget has shown, a new and more complex mental structure is elaborated and will evoke new intellectual possibilities. Children become capable of mental operations based on internal representations of external realities. That is to say, children begin to free themselves from concrete perceptions and to summon up awakening elements of autonomous thinking. This nascent functional skill shows up in the most diverse areas—logic, mathematics, physics, and geometry.

Children establish a new relationship with the parental world and with the physical and social environment. They die to their early childhood and open to a promise of new life. One of the most visible external signs of the five-year-old's transition is the loss of baby teeth. Many recall the first baby tooth falling out or being taken out, put under a cup or pillow, to be replaced the next morning by a coin.

Fordham (1969) reports that in certain tribes the first initiation takes place somewhere between four and twenty years old. And Henderson (1967) notes that dreams of an initiatory character may be observed long before adolescence. In the past in certain milieus, children who had reached the age of reason— around seven—set out for work. For example, in American society of the eighteenth and nineteenth centuries, the boy sometimes became a farm helper or apprentice, and the girl began to work as a domestic helper.

The five-year-old transition leading to the age of reason marks the beginning of an adventure that for many years will take the child on the road of life, the road of the world and of school, the road of human, material, and social accomplishments.

Strength, Openness, and Surrender

New situations that children face constantly call for a combined expression of their strength, openness, and capacity for surrendering. In the family, the children negotiate a place within the Oedipal triangle and among siblings. At school, they find a place among peers and in relationship to unfamiliar adults who are in positions of authority. Children also have to prove themselves in a highly competitive school system. Their daily interactions in familial and social contexts, and the physical surroundings, constantly test and develop the expression and assertion of their ego strength.

The evolution of consciousness passes through many stages. It progresses from the paradisal state of identity with the unconscious that characterizes the beginnings of life to a gradually more differentiated ego. In the beginning the ego is assimilated into and is identified with the unconscious, and emerges like an island of consciousness, at first intermittently and then for more sustained periods. To start with, the child does not have a stable separate ego or a definite body image. The child and the mother, and the child and the world, thus partake of the same biopsychic identity. Little by little the nucleus of the ego forms and implants itself toward the Self and toward the world in a polarized subject-object relationship. The development of the integrated, healthy ego is at the basis of the growth process. This integrity of the ego may require a struggle like that led by Eric with the psychic contents that his dream monsters represent, a struggle that shows his perseverance in assuring this integrity.

The development of ego strength, however, is constantly assisted and fortified by the ego's capacity for openness to and exchanges with what is other: the world, other human beings, ideas, and so on. If the child fights in order to assure a place in the sun of the familial constellation, the child's psychological survival is conceivable only with open and continual emotional exchanges with parents and with sisters and brothers. The nuclear family and the extended family constitute an organic and natural tissue enlivened by the quality and richness of its exchanges. Just as a microcosm reflects the organization of the macrocosm in which it is embedded, the intrapsychic structure of the child is strongly colored by the structure of the family into which the child is born and in which the child is raised.

Similarly, children more accurately perceive and more deeply meet and understand the new school environment when they have an openness for contacting other children and adults and for discovering new territories of knowledge toward which the school points them. The relating function leads to many territories of knowledge, since knowledge is also an expression of the relating function insofar as it is an encounter between mind and reality.

If the ego is formed by defining itself vis-à-vis another, and if it grows through interacting in an open manner with both physical reality and the human environment, then the ego also grows through exercising the power of surrender. This surrender, far from being a sign of passivity, actively involves the child with the forces of life. Such involvement, which is spontaneous for the child, first shows up in the child's natural play, a play that is a regenerating regression, a way of knowing, and a grace given childhood and life.

Surrender is also linked to a child's ability to feel the whole scale of emotions. Fear, anger, pleasure, pain, and enthusiasm constitute the raw material of the emotional life. The child's fear of the unknown, pain of failure, anger that shouts its demand for fairness, enthusiasm for discovering the surrounding world, and pleasure upon entering into life with all its high and low tides—all color the child's psychological reality.

Finally, surrender means losing, letting go, yielding, detaching, separating, and dying in order to be reborn to an incessantly new present. The Oedipal quest unavoidably implies loss as it comes up against the reality of the parental couple. Entering school means separating from the exclusive protection of the familial milieu. The first adventures outside the family bring their challenges and moments of disappointment. Growing up presupposes detaching from the state of childhood and from the privileges associated with it. And learning requires a constant giving up of insufficient notions and models so that new and more inclusive notions and models may be generated.

The first separations in childhood are often the occasion for wounds. The "complexes" that develop around these wounds, observes Verda Heisler,[5] are like sensitive and unconscious networks that affect the individual's expression of freedom in relating with others and the world. The "complexes" form from personal anecdotal events that the conscious memory forgets but that touch an archetypal core. This core may be recognized and encountered in adulthood, and can lead to recognition of a reality that lies deeper than the personal dimension and opens individuals to their totality.

The Initiating Function of the Monster

The monster may show itself in all areas in which the psychological universe of the child is growing and deepening. It looms up at the convergence between two planes of reality, one consisting in daily events and linked with the child's current life, the other intrapsychic and linked with the unconscious contents. It is easy to suppose that the monster in children's dreams represents parental figures, the rival parent in the Oedipal conflict or the all-powerful and punishing parent, or the overwhelming and devouring mother. Certain accounts of therapeutic interventions with children seem to indicate that, once unmasked, the monster in the dream of a child stands for the child's peer, such as a neighbor or schoolmate, and the fear that peer inspires (Cirincione et al. 1980).

The monster appearing in dreams may indeed be evoked by parental figures, as well as by peers or by any event that holds anxiety for the child, but the monster can never properly be reduced to only the people and events that evoke it. The monster refers to an unconscious content that at its deepest contains much more than personal figures whom it masks or behind which it hides.

In the dream series, the monster has by turns taken the form of the phantasmagorical being, the animal, and the human, as if embodied in more and more circumscribed but also more manageable forms, approaching the personal world of the dreamers. In Eric's series the monster went from phantasmagorical to animal form. In Pierre's it moved from phantasmagorical to animal, and to human with the woman who used the mirror. In Marjorie's the monster went from animal form to the human form of the monster-salesman. But just as psychological growth does not occur in a one-sided and even way but rather by leaps and bounds forward and relapses backward, so the sequence in these series does not develop through an orderly succession of forms. When the phantasmagorical monster recurs after the dream of the elephant in Eric's series, it has changed—it is now human-size and single. After Pierre has tamed the crocodile, the phantasmagorical monster returns, but then Pierre dispels it.

The forces that symbolize fire, water, the weapon, the sun's rays, and so on that appear in children's dreams sometimes serve the child and sometimes serve the monster. In Eric's series, for example, the fire is ignited through the magic of a triangle and it burns the monsters in the chimney; later it is a monster that sets Eric's house on fire. Similarly, Eric's ally Jos Lit pushes bullets into his body from a machine gun before confronting and devouring the monsters; in a later dream, the machine gun is used by the enemy monster against Eric's house. In a drawing by Pierre the sun's rays kill the maniac who threatens "a little boy"; later, the woman with the mirror catches the solar rays and provokes fainting in those at whom she directs the rays. In all of these instances, there is a dynamic interplay between child and monster, between strategies that assist one and that assist the other, as if an ongoing intrapsychic process has emerged from the interactional dynamic between child and monster.

The monster appearing in dreams is both universal and eminently individual. The crocodile that appears in Eric's series, for instance, is not identical to the crocodile in Pierre's dream. Each is defined by the totality of the context in which it is inscribed, including the attitude of the child-dreamer. The crocodile in Eric's dream is in a cage. Eric is separated from it by a river and he throws a stone at it. The crocodile in Pierre's dream is in the child's bedroom. Discovering the animal, Pierre decides to caress it, prompting the crocodile to metamorphose into a small and gentle animal. A symbol is not an interchangeable abstraction: although the number one and the number one are identical, the crocodile in Eric's dream and the crocodile in Pierre's dream are not.

The monster and the dreamer form a distinctive organic configuration. The crocodile in Eric's dream remains a cold character whom Eric keeps at a distance and whom he attacks with a weapon. The crocodile in Pierre's dream presents itself in the intimate surrounding of the child's bedroom. Pierre approaches it with his bare hands and tames it by caressing it. The relationship between the child and the animal soul to which the crocodile gives form differs from one dreamer to the next, and the crocodile behaves like a different character in the two series.

The monster is a numinous and unknown power, and when the monster appears on the child's path, it stimulates the child to become centered and to experience and mobilize his or her own strength. The monster is also a being of metamorphosis, awakening the child who approaches it with the intelligence of the heart to that child's own creative openness and relational function. The monster finally is the engulfer, the one who swallows and brings renewed life, and it initiates the one who descends to its depths into the mystery of surrender and the perpetual regeneration of life.

The monster who appears in the child's dream is a natural phenomenon of psychological life with its own laws. And if the monster is experienced as a threat to the ego of the growing child, it may also spur the development of that ego, reinforcing its strength, favoring its openness or regenerating it, as the child encounters the monster and becomes immune to its dangers by taking in infinitesimal doses the psychic force to which the monster gives form.

Female Initiation, Male Initiation

Tangible differences between boys and girls have been identified at each stage of this study. First, the analysis of dream contents has revealed differences in the themes and settings of the dreams of each sex. In boys, the themes of the phantasmagorical monster and water dominated, whereas in girls those of the animal and the earth dominated. In dreams of boys and girls, the animal was likened to the monster due to its function as a threatening dream figure, but not in an exclusive way. In girls' dreams, for example, the animal theme was also linked to themes of family life and fertility. Boys' dreams principally were set in the intimacy of the home, but girls' dreams had natural outdoors settings.[6] In response to challenges, boys were more inclined to adopt active measures, whereas the dreams of the girls carried motifs of symbolic death or loss, such as dying in a car accident, being robbed of one's jewelry, being eaten, and losing personal objects.

An analysis of the strategies for encountering the monster also showed appreciable differences in child-monster-strategy configurations. The dreams of boys contained a larger array of fighting strategies. To these were added active strategies for approaching and exploring the monster. Boys' strategies included recourse to an ally, to magic, and to weapons. Girls' dreams had few scenes of conflict, and in these scenes cunning was sometimes used. New strategies arose, however, including elimination of the malefic power of the monster, surrender to engulfment, and care for oneself after being wounded. And the adult ally also performed new functions: the father carried the child in his arms while escaping with her, the mother consoled her, the father showed her which way to behave with crocodiles.

The three series described the dream experience of two boys and one girl, and these series reflect how activity predominates for the two boys. In Eric's and Pierre's series, despite the individuality of their styles, the active nature of their involvement shines through, whether the activity reacts to the presence of the monster or comes from the children's own initiative. All of Eric's strategies were oriented to active struggling with the monster. He pushed the monsters into the chimney and, through the intermediary of his imaginary companion, bested and devoured them. Pierre's activity took the form of approaching the monster, pursuing his curiosity, touching the monster, helping the monster to emerge and change, and finally taming the monster. In both series, the activity was displayed outwardly and its goal was explicit. These forms of activity easily lend themselves to description.

For Marjorie, by contrast, the series unraveled as if in silence, and meaningful gestures spoke instead of valiant activities. Marjorie entered into the belly of the whale. She climbed upon the cross. After the dog had bitten her, she took care of herself. Face to face with the monster-salesman, she spoke. These are Marjorie's gestures, filled with meaning. Marjorie simply goes into the belly of the whale, with no additional conspicuous or describable action. The outcome of Pierre's taming is visible in the dream itself, for the crocodile metamorphoses into a small and gentle animal. The combat in Eric's dreams also reaches endings in the dreams themselves. The monster is evacuated from the house, knocked down or eaten up. But the outcome of Marjorie's engulfment is not apparent in the dream and its meaning as a gesture is paradoxical if considered from the masculine point of view focused on external and explicit activity. From the perspective of masculine consciousness, the engulfment appears as if Marjorie had failed in action. But it is not so. The engulfment marks the passage to another plane. It is an opening into activity of an entirely different nature, a more interior and spiritual activity, which cannot be understood except in light of a symbolic approach that seeks out its meanings.

The series of Eric, Pierre, and Marjorie probably express their individuality, reflect their tasks for growing up at the time the dreams were collected, and also exhibit their innate as well as culturally influenced male and female status and circumstances.

Marjorie's series is of particular interest. It speaks to the process of psychological development in the girl and the symbolic forms by which that development progresses. Description of the psychological development of the child has generally been made by male theoreticians from the point of view of the boy. Freud's Oedipal theory, for example, is conceived from the boy's point of view and applied to the girl by the extension of a simple reciprocity. In *The Child* (1973), Neumann describes, from the male point of view, the phases through which the child emerges and evolves. According to him, development proceeds from a matriarchal phase to a patriarchal phase, and then to a phase centered on the group, and then to individuation. In his view, the development of both sexes is identical in the first stages. One may wonder if this is so. Neumann died before finishing his work and he never approached the specific development of the girl, as he had planned.

The female's development in symbolic form awaits further elaboration. For Marjorie this includes the themes of the voyage, the engulfment, the ocean, the mountain, the dropped child, the house that burns, the violence from males, the walk in the night, the unknown savior, the rebirth, and many others. Other girls' dreams furnish other motifs—of the family, animal fertility, stolen jewelry, the celebration of marriage, venturing into the jungle and meeting the serpent, the "Bionic" girl who cuts wood for a man, the lost child, the beautiful house, the captured bird, and the hydra flower. Each of these motifs would yield valuable understanding of the female child's quest for growth.

The combat of the hero with the monster, prominent in Eric's series, is a highly active motif in the imagination of boys. The auxiliary motifs—the paternal ally, the comrade-in-arms, the weapon, the deployment of active force and aggression, the putting to death of the enemy—are all present in the constellation of the warrior-hero.

The taming of the monster that culminates Pierre's approach and active exploration brings to light another dimension of the psychological experience of the boy. The taming, which operates under the magic of the creative power and the intelligence of the heart, elicits the relational function, leading to the transformation of the monster instead of its death. In Pierre's series the female figures appear as the one to whom the hero brings the fruits of victory, the unknown and terrible woman, the ally against the monster, and the monster's victim—revealing the child's active and complex relationship with the mother and with the feminine.

The integral development of the child requires the inclusion of all three dynamic functions toward which the series point: could the contact with a deep movement of life that Marjorie's odyssey suggests be balanced by the ability to approach people, objects, ideas, and situations with openness and to mobilize her active force? Could Pierre's creative, open, often experimental approach be balanced by direct confrontation and affirmation of his truth? Could Eric's combative perseverance make room at the opportune moment for surrender and openness?

As dynamic functions, strength, openness, and surrender are independent of gender. Strength is as much a girl's privilege and power as a boy's, and openness and creative surrender are also the prerogative of both sexes. But culturally, combat is associated with the masculine principle, even while it is active in both sexes. Surrender is generally associated with the feminine principle, but it shows up in both sexes. Openness or the relational function, also associated with the feminine principle, finds its expression in both sexes.

The expression of feminine and masculine archetypes is always colored by a specific cultural context. Garfield (1984) notes that the weapon motif, for example, consisting in guns, swords, arrows, boomerangs, and so on, is more clearly marked in American boys than in boys from India. In eighteen dreams coming from eight American boys between the ages of five and eight, she counted thirteen references to weapons and only five in the fifty-two dreams reported by seven Indian boys between the ages of six and twelve. American culture, and more generally Western culture, is strongly influenced by the masculine principle and patriarchal consciousness, whereas Indian society is decidedly less influenced, or influenced in a different way.

For the needs of collective humanity, diversity may serve better than homogeneity. Differences between the sexes, among different types within each sex, and ultimately differences among individuals with a unique combination of strength, openness, and surrender may benefit humanity more than one particular ideal turned into a standard of value. If an integrated development tends toward including the three functions represented by combat, taming, and engulfment, we may ask if the way to wholeness follows distinct sequences for each sex. There may also be a masculine power different from a feminine power, and a girl's quest may express itself in symbolic forms differing from a boy's.

The fundamental question of the genesis of female and male initiation is vivid in our culture. We are now at the heart of a deep mutation in our collective awareness of the feminine and the masculine. We give form to new and more encompassing models, models that are more diverse and flexible. This movement toward the freeing of gender-identified categories from traditional restrictions supports a realization of our common humanity more fully enabled to participate together in collective life. And the quest of the child for development is inscribed in this movement.

From Childhood to Adulthood

Childhood from birth to age seven corresponds to the first cycle of life. Passage to the age of reason at age seven ends this cycle, but all the other cycles along the spiral of development unfold upon it.

The study of the all-powerful monster that strikes the child dumb, of the monster metamorphosed into its opposite by the magic of the intelligence of the heart, and of the monster that swallows and contains one is a study that commences a contemplation of mysteries. These mysteries are *tremendum*, Eros, and death and rebirth. These mysteries point to forces of life that govern human development from birth to death. Personal encounters with *tremendum*, with Eros, and with death and rebirth are encounters that change and deepen from one cycle of life to the next.

The first intimations of *tremendum* in childhood come in striking dreams, numinous sensations, and preoccupations with questions of life and death, questions concerning the nature of the universe and "the existence of God." These intimations can constitute the first steps toward an adult relationship with the sacred. First intimations of Eros come from those first experiences of love in childhood, the love of one's mother and father. This love echoes in the adolescent awakening to love, in the adult experience of loving relations, and in the universal compassion of the mature being. The wounds of childhood, the feelings of loss and rejection, of surrender, and the first deaths and renewals all serve as the raw material out of which an adult can later forge the intention to gain inner freedom.

Children, adolescents, and adults are capable of different degrees of conscious participation in the transition from one cycle of life to another, and the specific meanings of each transition also vary. But the structure of the psychic processes at work, and the symbolic forms through which these processes express themselves, seem to recur. For the sake of each transition an as-yet unknown difficulty arises, and for the sake of each transition one must die to an old way of being in the world in order to be born into a new way of being. The passage of the five-year-old from one cycle to another resonates with the shape, the meaning, and the purposes of all the other cycles on the spiral of human development.

Chapter Nine

Steps toward Oneiric Education

The educational practice of the Malaysian Senoi, who teach their children "the art of dreaming," inspired this study. At the time Herbert Noone discovered the Senoi in the early 1930s, this aboriginal people was just beginning to have contact with industrial civilization.[1] The Senoi at that time lived in a dense and luxuriant jungle, and they had never seen the ocean.

Noone was the first to study the Senoi and to have ongoing contact with them. Other scientists followed after him. Then the war came, and during the Japanese occupation of Malaysia some British took refuge in the jungle. But Communist Chinese guerrillas were also hiding in the jungle. The Senoi first served the British cause and later the cause of the Chinese Communists. The Senoi had a profound knowledge of the jungle, which made them invaluable allies for any group forced to withdraw to this unfamiliar territory. At the end of the war, the liberation gradually returned the jungle to the Senoi, and the government put medical and educational services at their disposal (Noone 1972).

The Senoi still live in the jungle in their traditional longhouses, although some of them live on the fringe of the jungle in government-built settlements, generally a cluster of shacks around a single building functioning as store, school, and community center. Visitors who come into contact with them continue to be touched by their proverbial amiability. But the Senoi now have to cope with the values and sometimes the pressures of the government and the surrounding civilization; and, according to Alexander Randall (1983), the practice of the art of dreaming and the teaching of this art to Senoi children might also be in the process of becoming lost.[2]

At the time Herbert Noone encountered the Senoi, the dream was at the heart of their spiritual life. The spiritual and social life of this people, as well

105

as their relationship with nature, partook of the same spiritual vision. This vision was shared by the whole group.

In comparison with the Senoi, we live in an extremely heterogeneous society. Furthermore, in our modern world the spiritual, political, and social realms are dissociated, while our relationships with nature, the body, and the earth express attitudes that are materialistic and desacralized.

The discovery of the educational practice of the Senoi has renewed our thinking about children's dreams. The contact with a shamanic approach to dreams, which the Senoi oneiric practice exemplifies, has had the vitalizing effect on our modern sensibilities of a return to the source. But if the Senoi approach could stimulate our imagination and help us catch a glimpse of the potential of dreams, we must now let a vision of oneiric education emerge that takes our Western contemporary reality into account. For this we must turn to our dreams and the dreams of our children. We must reclaim our spiritual inheritance as expressed through the ages in symbols and myths. Finally, we must strive to recover a unified vision of reality that may, perhaps, only be accomplished by recovering a sense of the sacred.

Letting the Dreams of Children Educate Us

The time that I devoted to living with the dreams of children, to letting these dreams impregnate me, to hearing the dream symbols in their deepest and most intimate sonorities, has been a real education. In the universe of dreams, there is no space for answers that have been established in advance or that are identical for everyone. The richness of dreams constantly places in the researcher's path new challenges, calling each time for unique responses adapted to the specific situation of a given dreamer and to the context of a particular dream.

Children's dreams give expression to contents that unavoidably bring us face to face with the unknown. In theory, the contents that can appear in the dreams of children extend to the limits of the psyche itself. Thus they have the breadth of a whole universe. And faced with this universe, we are in the position of a scientist asking questions about unknown phenomena, observing those phenomena, and forming hypotheses as explanations, but ready to abandon these hypotheses when the data disconfirm them.

In addition, since the child brings a certain innocence to the facts of a dream, we may be more worried or embarrassed by the contents of a dream than the child. We may recall the end of one dream, when Eric says to his mother, who is astounded to see the monster under him, "Of course! There's always a monster under me." Eric's words reflect both the gap that may sometimes exist between the adult's and the child's perception and the child's awareness of this gap.

As a consequence, it can be important for us to distinguish between our own emotional reactions to the child's dream contents and the child's experience, and thereby prevent our reactions from forming a barrier between child and dream. We may, however, be puzzled or intrigued by a particular dream and fruitfully carry it around inside ourselves, seeing what meanings it suggests after a time, and becoming receptive to perceptions and associations that the dream evokes. In some instances we can add to this intuitive approach by using other resources, such as accounts of myths, fairy tales, and rituals, which increase our understanding of dream symbols. But above all we can receive instruction from the child directly, observing the child's relation to the dream, following the developments in later dreams, and listening to what the child says about them.

It is to our advantage to school ourselves in the dreams of children, to recognize their dream experience, to observe its movements and appreciate the intelligence it expresses. To do this we must approach children's dreams with fresh eyes, free from preestablished systems of interpretation, and prepare to be moved, astonished, and instructed by the dreams themselves.

Until now the dreams of children have remained hidden in the silence of night. But more and more educational projects focused on children's dreams are being undertaken. Some of these projects aim at the development of the imaginative life and the creativity of children (Jones 1971; Koch 1970; Werlin 1967). Others, which are inspired by Senoi educational practices, explore the use of alternate endings to dreams (DeClerque 1978; Hudson and O'Connor 1981; Garfield 1984). Gradually the curtain of silence lifts from the oneiric life of children, and we begin to hear that life.

It is difficult to conceive of oneiric education without cultivating our relationship as adults to our own dreams. More than anything else, it is the quality of our own relationship to dreams that children learn, and with our recognition of dreams as valid and relevant on a daily basis for an integrated life. The contact with symbolic life through dreams adds another dimension to human experience, rooting it in the deeper zones of the psyche and connecting it to a living source. Symbols are forms of psychic energy that, when approached, met, and assimilated, may give vitality to the child or adult dreamer and serve the growth of that dreamer.

It is also through our own experience that we find the sensitivity needed for listening to and understanding the dream of another, and believing in it. While dreams are always present on the threshold of our days, it remains for us to direct our attention toward them. It remains for us to observe the scenarios of our dreams, the characters that throng them, the symbols that speak in them, the places they occur, and to identify the challenges with which they confront us and our ways of encountering those challenges. We can learn the language of dreams as if we were learning a new language or rather, making contact again with an ancient, concrete, and universal form of expression.

Opportunities abound for becoming acquainted with the reality of dreams. There are workshops and groups on dreams, therapeutic approaches that recognize the significance of dreams, and a considerable number of books on dreams. And anyone can keep a dream journal.

Guiding Children in the Art of Dreaming

Often we conceive of education only as intervention and forget the receptivity that precedes and gives birth to intervention. Dreams are part of children's individual lives, but by receptive empathy we can attune ourselves to children's dreams, become lucid and sensitive witnesses who are able to receive children's oneiric experience and, if the privilege is granted us, guide children in "the art of dreaming."

The context we create in which to approach the dreams of children has much significance and influence. We must use our time to become available if we want the relationship with oneiric life to grow and bear fruit. Such a context always has the contours of a given place, time, and ritual, varying according to different settings, such as family, school, or therapy.

In a family setting, dreams can be shared in the morning when the child awakens with a dream, or at breakfast, or in a calm period after the evening meal. In her educational experience with a small group of seven to eight children, Caroline DeClerque (1978) sat in a rocking chair and listened to the dreams of children. In my study, the room in which we withdrew from the larger class, the table at which we sat, our spontaneous exchanges, the recording and drawing of the dreams—all contributed to the context in which dreams could be explored. Certain gestures and objects take on the function of establishing passage from daily life to the context devoted to dreams.

Our role as it relates to the dreams of children is limited to a large extent to that of a witness to their oneiric processes. These oneiric processes have their own movement. Symbols give form to unconscious contents, which in turn put an impetus into the psychic life of the dreamer. In children, this impetus may lead to direct activity playing out the dream. Thus children sometimes spontaneously replay and develop dreams over many weeks and months, as we can see from the dream series.

The primary meaning of witness is one who sees or hears something and can attest to it. But here, witness is defined as one who participates with receptivity and sensitivity in the experience of another.

In collecting the dreams of children, my intervention was generally limited to questions aimed at clarifying the content described by the child, or getting information on the emotion the child felt upon awakening from the dream. I provided a setting in which a psychic process could occur and develop. My task consisted in being present to this process and discovering it from moment to moment as it unfolded.

In her therapeutic use of sand play with children and adults, Dora Kalff (1980) used a sand tray (fifty-seven by seventy-two by seven centimeters) with a large tray of toy figures, including animals, human characters, trees, vehicles, and mythic beings. With the toy figures, the child or adult creates a three-dimensional picture in the sand. The sand tray delineates a space that Kalff conceives of as "a sacred space," that is, a *temenos*. The Greek word *temenos* designates a "piece of land dedicated to the gods" or "a sacred precinct." Within this precinct, a psychic process occurs that Kalff witnesses with receptivity and empathy similar to that in my definition of witness. This essentially receptive form of participation can function as a catalyst for the child's psychic process.

Dreams pertain to a child's individual life and thus must be approached with respect. Certain dreams with numinous symbols are like a fertilization, and it is only through time that this fertilization will activate psychic processes and lead to a development of parts of the child's life. Often children have an instinctive appreciation for the value of their private life and the sacred. A seven-year-old girl got up one morning and told her father, "Last night, I had the most beautiful dream of my whole life, but I'm not going to tell you." And the girl went away as if protecting a secret treasure.

There are manners we must practice with respect to our dreams and with the dreams of children, and these manners include the guarding of a certain silence: "There are many people," observes von Franz, "who have some great experience which somehow is swept away again. They have not recognized and accepted it, and realized that they had to do so. The moral obligations of gratitude do not only apply to our society but also to that of the Gods. The inner factors also have the right to the human attitude of gratitude and loyalty and of abiding by the experience. People lose that in moods and extraversion and do not feel the obligation" (von Franz 1980c, 156).

Silence functions as an alchemical container protecting the creative processes still incubating. Individual and group work with children's dreams will always have the limitations that recognition and respect for intimacy and privacy imposes. Whether in an individual or a group setting, it is important that children know that if they have the opportunity to tell a dream, they also have the privilege to keep silent.

The entrance into night and the descent into sleep mark a passage for which children prepare themselves through a whole array of gestures and rituals that sometimes almost seem like ceremonials. The child demands that the mother or father be present at a certain place, that they sing a particular song, tell a story, take the child in their arms, kiss the child a certain number of times, or recite some ritual formula. Some children go to sleep while sucking their thumbs, while others need a piece of cotton or cloth, to which they are uniquely attached, to hold in their hand or rub on their faces. Still others play with a lock of hair or sleep with a teddy bear that cannot be taken from them or even moved (Ajuriaguerra 1974).

These "sleeping rituals" of children, which Julián de Ajuriaguerra likens to "conjuratory rites against anxiety" (190), resemble certain practices found in the accounts of various cultures, practices used to protect people against "the demons of the night." These include protective prayers uttered upon waking at the place one has dreamed, magical formulas and purification rituals with specific gestures for the task of climbing out of bed. In Egypt on the headboards of beds were carved the figure of a protecting god piercing a ghost or demon with arrows, and in China a similarly placed figure of a mythic animal is depicted devouring "evil dreams" (Monneret 1976).

It is important to send children into the night with warm feelings and with a sense of security and wishes for meaningful dreams, for to dream well is also to live well.

Telling the Dream

Adults are sometimes confronted by the anxiety that children with bad dreams or nocturnal fears experience—a witch seeps through the window, gnomes sneak out through cracks in the wall, there is a ghost in the closet, the child has dreamed of a wolf. Children's dreams must be received without reduction. The psychic experience that dreams send may be very vivid, even if they occur in another domain of reality, and for the young child who receives such dreams, this domain feels real.

Adults with emotional warmth are the first allies of a child facing a traumatic dream or a nocturnal fear. It may happen that the child spontaneously takes refuge in a parent's bedroom or that the child's crying calls out to a parent or parents. In these states of fear breathing is affected and perceptions are sometimes distorted. The parent may invite the child to breathe slowly and deeply to help the child calm down, soothe the child by touching the child's hand or forehead, hug the child, or rub the child's back. The qualities in the voice that the parent uses to speak to the child may also help if its sound is low-pitched and confident. Finally, a parent may use a familiar song or verbal formula that gives the child a sense of safety. And the parent can listen to the child's dream: "What have you dreamed? And what else?" all the way to the end of the dream. At school, in therapy, in the research laboratory, a benevolent adult is also the child's first ally.

Telling one's dream is an act with an aim of its own. The ancients believed that telling one's dream was a way of exorcising it and that telling a dream sufficed for being free of the evil in it (Monneret 1976). Telling one's dream objectifies it. The dream is then perceived as an element outside the dreamer, and its contours gain in precision and definition. In telling her or his dream the child gains some distance from the event of the dream, and the child is no longer alone with the emotional charge that the dream carries.

The key to a dream resides in its content. This content, with its many elements, must be considered in several ways. Does the child dream of a fire, an accident, a wolf? Does the child dream of falling into emptiness? Does he or she hear a strange sound? Is the child coping with a threatening character; a phantasmagorical being; an animal, crocodile, or spider; a human being, female or male? Where is the dream taking place? What is the strategy to which the boy or girl dreamer has recourse? Does the child cry, call for help, try to struggle? Does the child-dreamer escape or defend herself or himself? Does the child cope alone, or with the assistance of an ally? Is the ally an adult, a relative, an unknown character? Is the ally a peer of the child's, a female friend, a brother? What are the resources the dream conceals that could lead the way to resolution? The needed help can sometimes come from an element of nature or from an object. The snake that was chasing Françoise, for example, lost track of her when it entered the water and found something else to eat besides Françoise. A small floating bench was in the river into which Jacques fell.

It is unavoidable that children and adults have anxiety-filled dreams occasionally. These are particularly likely to emerge at the point of transition from one life phase to another, since, as Neumann (1973) suggested, "Each time that the ego is forced to abandon its previous position, it is assailed by fear" (168). Some children are sensitive to the processes of the unconscious, and they have a rich and active dream life. Others are compelled to pay attention to their dreams because their dreams recur. Such children gain from being accompanied by an adult through their difficulties and beyond, to a more fulfilling oneiric life.

The territory of this oneiric life, however, is not limited to dreams of shadow and challenge, for it also includes luminous or simply favorable dreams that stimulate or inspire the life of the children who dream them. Some of these dreams are about performance. Thus Marjorie dreamed of being able to ride a two-wheeled bicycle. Michel dreamed of going to the skating rink and of shooting his hockey puck into the goal. Other happy dreams involved beautiful houses, life with friends, lucky finds. Marie dreamed of a magnificent house. In her drawing she represented the house in white with large windows on the second floor and on the ground level.

Jacques dreamed that he met his pal Robert and that around them there were many beautiful houses "of all colors." His was the most beautiful house; when Jacques entered it he discovered many "sport cars." Then Jacques went to school. But the school was larger than in waking reality and it also was made "of all colors." Robert was "all dressed for winter," whereas Jacques wore "only light clothing." Jacques said to Robert: "Take off your big winter coat, it's much too hot, it's summer." Jacques's dream probably portrays the euphoria inspired by the first signs of spring after a long winter (see fig. 16).

Hélène's beneficent dream spoke of feasting, an abundant table, and marriage. Hélène dreamed that she was a bride and that for the marriage supper the wedding party ate lobster and shrimp, and that afterward they went dancing (see fig. 17).

The numinous dreams of childhood remain alive in the dreamer's mind sometimes even into adulthood. A thirty-two-year-old man still remembers a dream he had when he was five years old in which he was riding along the ocean shore mounted on a superb white horse. He was naked on his horse and he had long blond hair flowing down to his shoulders. Often a "beautiful dream" is a happy event not only for the dreamer but for all those to whom it is told.

Some dreamers, children or adults, have to learn to direct their attention to the aspects of their dreams that are fertile, redemptive, and luminous in order to realize that the oneiric territory is larger, more generous, and more diverse than it originally appeared.

A Child's Strategies for Coping

The strategies children use for coping with psychic contents may have their origins in psychic patterns discernible in dreams, myths, and fairy tales. But these more general strategies soon acquire individual qualities. They develop, diversify, and become refined as the relationship with intrapsychic life develops. It is usually better to support children in solving for themselves the challenges that oneiric life presents, and to support them in contacting their own inner resources so that they can develop these strategies.

This study has shown that children who did not receive any oneiric education were not without "art" in their oneiric practice. In their dreams, we have seen them move toward the discovery of what intrigued them, fight when they were under the threat of a phantasmagorical or animal monster, receive help from allies who were adults or peers. The child-dreamers have shown themselves to be participating subjects, actively engaged in their oneiric processes, and not just passive victims of their dreams.

The reading of dreams in a series has also shown that a given dreamer employed a large diversity of strategies. These strategies varied from one dream to the next. Pierre, for example, fled from the phantasmagorical monster of his dream, and later, by touching it, he dispelled the monster who changed into many colors. In one dream, he tamed a crocodile, and in another he awoke in order to escape from the woman with the mirror. A strategy always

Figure 16. Drawing 24" x 18". From left to right: the school and six houses of all colors. Center foreground: Jacques and his friend Robert.

Figure 17. Drawing 18" x 12". The marriage, with festive decorations and Hélène as a bride.

comes at a significant moment in the course of the oneiric process, and strategies change throughout the series of dreams, as do the challenges that call them forth.

A dreamer's strategy can only be fully appreciated in the setting in which it occurs, and this setting includes not only the dream series itself but also the personality of the dreamer and the nature of the challenge confronted. A strategy always reflects both the dreamer and the challenge, and it is simultaneously defined by one and the other.

Finally, our culture carries with it some sexist valuations that may obscure the value of the differing strategies of children of each sex. Boys' generally more active strategies are likely to attract attention more immediately. The sometimes more discrete strategies of girls deserve to be fully understood and equally appreciated for the potential they bear.

Oneiric contents give form to psychic energies of quite different natures. There are a diversity of dreams and so there cannot be a simple and univocal way of coping with the dream contents that children encounter. All the complexity of psychic reality is reflected in children's dreams. We also find an expression of this complexity in fairy tales. Having studied fairy tales for many years, Marie-Louise von Franz (1974) has attempted to discern in them general rules of human behavior, perhaps simple, but valid beyond individual and national differences. But she has not found them. The wisdom of fairy tales, on the contrary, shows how contradictory and situation-governed the "rules" appear to be:

> I have looked at collective fairy tale material for many years, wondering whether it would be possible to find a few general rules of human behavior which would always be valid. I was fascinated by the idea of finding some generally human code, simple, but beyond national and individual differentiations, some kind of basic rule of human behavior. I have to confess that I have not found a standard basic rule, or rather, I have found it and I have not found it, for there is always a contradiction!
>
> I can tell you stories which say that if you meet evil you must fight it, but there are just as many which say that you must run away and not try to fight it. Some say to suffer without hitting back, others say don't be a fool, hit back! There are stories which say that if you are confronted with evil the only thing to do is lie your way out of it; others say no, be honest, even towards the devil, don't become involved with lying. For all these I will give you examples, but it is always a Yes and a No, there are just as many stories which say the one as the other. It is a complete *complexio oppositorum*, which simply means that, *post eventum*, I disappointedly came to the conclusion that really it *should* be like that, because it is *collective* material! How, otherwise, could there be individual action? (119)

Thus in dreams there are circumstances in which the confrontation with a threatening figure is required, and others in which taming is in harmony with the intelligence of the dream. There are conditions in which recourse to an ally proves to be the most responsible way to proceed, and others in which the dreamer is called to act alone. There are moments in which fleeing might be the chosen method, or in which caring for oneself after having been wounded is appropriate.

Dreaming calls for lucidity in the present. Each challenge encountered in oneiric life claims a response that is adapted to the specific nature of the situation presented by the dream. And as dream situations diversify, dreamers' ability to mobilize themselves and act in harmony with the intelligence of the dream also increases.

Alternate Endings for Dreams

In order to guide children, adults will have to rely in part on their own common sense and wisdom. With a young child, the situation may require confronting waking reality—checking "the window through which dreams enter," the closet that seems inhabited, the area under the bed where a crocodile might be swimming. In accompanying children in these ways, adults communicate to them that they take the children's experience seriously, and they offer them the opportunity to explore reality safely and to find out for themselves. Furthermore, action is movement, and as such it can function as an antidote to the paralyzing inhibition children's fears induce and can help children to conquer that fear.

Sometimes the most natural thing to do is to join children in their magical thinking: "If the witch comes back again, wind up your musical lamb and the music will drive her away." In addition to enlisting the magical thinking of the child, this suggestion of a mother to her three-year-old son also conferred a protective function on the child's toy. In antiquity, toys offered to children were also charms or amulets aimed at protecting them from malevolent influences. But in other cases it might be appropriate to explore alternate solutions to the dream, asking the child: "If the dream returns, what could you do? How could you solve the problem? Is there something or someone who could help you in your dream? Do you know that you can try to defend yourself in your dream?"

In her work of educating seven to eight children about dreams, DeClerque (1978) led children age six to eight to explore alternative endings to their dreams. She asked the children to describe the content of their dreams, the person or the animal that chased them and she listened for cues that could give hints about new ways of coping with the dream's dilemma. The following example illustrates her interaction with Jane, an eight-year-old girl who dreamed of being squashed in the scree off a mountain:

J: Well, you see...I was in Colorado.

C: You were in Colorado.

J: Yup. And we were at the bottom of the mountain and these boulders just on the edge of the mountain...and they started rolling...like it was alive. And I said, "Look out, Daddy." He said, "Oh no!"

C: He could see it too? ´

J: And we couldn't get away. And the boulder got that close to us. (She holds her hands about a foot apart.)

C: Oh.

J: And the boulder went right over us.

C: And the boulder went right over you and then...did you wake up?

J: I felt all squashed when I woke up.

C: You felt all squashed when you woke up. And...but were you able to breathe?

J: Yeah.

C: I wonder what would have happened if you hadn't gotten awake at that moment...

J: I wouldn't wake up till next year.

C: ...if you went right on dreaming it at that time and didn't wake up as the boulder went over you.

J: I would have to wake up. My mother waked me up.

C: Oh. Your mother woke you up. Was that the end of the dream?

J: Yeah.

C: What I am trying to say is that sometimes if...when you have a scary part of your dream...if you don't wake up at that time, but go on dreaming...and call on some dream friends...you had your daddy to call on...to help you...

J: He didn't do a thing....The thing that is going to help me is the mountain...

C: The mountain might help you.

J: ...the only thing it did wrong...it shook.

C: Since you created the dream, maybe next time you can have it not shake.

(66–68)

Solutions imagined by children can astonish us sometimes. In other circumstances, DeClerque asked the children to play the dream scenes and to embody one protagonist after another. She invited the children to dance their dreams, to render their dreams through music, painting, drawing, or sculpture.

There are cases in which it might be advisable to accompany a child through the territory of the dream with active imagination. The dreamer then enters the dream again by visualization and lets the dream develop. In the following example, Leonard Handler (1972) taught an eleven-year-old boy to come to grips with a recurring dream and to confront the monster of his nights. Handler himself modeled the behavior to be adopted toward the monster.

Handler asked the child to visualize the monster in front of him and then took the initiative in sending the monster away with these words: "Get out of here, you lousy monster, leave my friend John alone! Get away, stay away."

Then Handler invited the child to join him in the confrontation with the monster, which the child did timidly at first, but then with more and more intensity and confidence. Handler and the child went over the same procedure again, but in the dark. Handler encouraged the child to use this strategy if the monster showed up again in his dream, a strategy that the child had occasion to use later, successfully.

For Mary Arnold-Forster, an explorer of dreams at the beginning of this century, the first step in coping with "bad dreams" is not to explore alternate endings to dreams but to learn to awaken from them at will. In her book *Studies in Dreams* (1921), Arnold-Forster observed that adults could easily teach young children simple methods of dream control that allowed them to gain power over their nocturnal phantasms: "If a child once knows that he is not defenceless, and that he possesses in his own will-power a real and efficient weapon against his bad dreams, he will assuredly learn how to use it. You give him hope, and you take away from him the paralysing sense of helplessness that is almost the worst part of the trouble" (32). Although willpower does not always work, Arnold-Forster recommended using a verbal formula as short and simple as possible, one that the child repeats often, especially before going to bed, until the words become so familiar that they spontaneously enter the child's mind when the child has a "bad dream." This formula, for example, might be, "This is only a dream—it must stop."

Arnold-Forster suggested teaching children this dream control method by using a story about fictional children coming to grips with a problem of "bad dreams." And she added that these fictional children, whose oneiric adventures we tell, should not only learn to master their "bad dreams" but should go further, discovering the pleasure of dream adventures and dream travel, and also the joy of learning how to fly.

Amplifying Children's Dreams

Dreams are not only settings where describable actions occur, they are also replete with symbolic meanings. These meanings emerged in the dream series of Eric, Pierre and Marjorie and shed light on the dreamers' actions. By focusing only on the activities of the dreamer and neglecting the larger symbolic function of dreams, the riches in depth and understanding of children's dreams are lost.

Dreams may always be read on more than one level simultaneously. Dreams have an anecdotal or subjective dimension associated with the current events in the dreamer's life. The link between a dream and a child's daily life comes to prominence sometimes when the child tells or draws his or her dream. Children, for example, may give unknown characters in their dreams the names of people whom they know from neighborhood or school life.

Even if the character from the dream with a similar name cannot be reduced to the person from the child's waking life, some association may enrich
the meaning. And it might be appropriate to explore what transpired between the child and the person in the child's waking life, what the child felt
around the person, and how the child behaved with that person. This type
of exploration of the child's life context starting from the child's dream is a
subjective amplification of the dream.

We can also trace the meanings of dream symbols through the use of
theoretical or objective points of view, as I did in approaching the dream series.
The symbols and motifs that appear in children's dreams are often to be found
in fairy tales, myths, art, and children's literature. It can sometimes be meaningful for children to find the symbol or motif of a dream that intrigues or
worries them somewhere in a parallel context. For that matter, children's
literature abounds in many types of works, including picture books, illustrated
tales, comic books, books that tell about and document animals, monsters,
ancient art, and history. In perceiving a symbol or an oneiric motif in the
light of a parallel context, children multiply their points of view on this symbol or motif, and their experience of them is thus enlarged.

A child who had a recurring vampire dream tamed her fear by reading all
that she could on the subject, which fascinated her. Her exploration of the
theme of the vampire offered an outlet for her feelings and helped her explore the meanings of her dream in other contexts.

A story that treats a theme in a child's dream can also allow a child to en-
vison a way of resolving the problem in the dream.

Our recognition of the meaning with which a dream functions does not
justify offering an interpretation of children's dreams to children. As Richard
M. Jones noted, "The surest way to discourage children from sharing their
dreams is to interpret them" (1971, 97). What is important is to encourage
children to live their dreams, to permit them to tame their dreams by telling
them, to inhabit their dreams more deeply by expressing them in drawing,
sculpture, movement, dramatic play, and sound. And it is important to offer
children the opportunity to continue their dreams by using some form of active imagination, to see their dreams anew in the light of parallel contexts.
These practices constitute ways of guiding children in the art of dreaming.

Work with children's dreams will always have its limitations. There are
dreams that adults never hear about. A twenty-six-year-old poet recalls that
her childhood sleep was often visited by visions of gnomes about which she
did not dare tell her parents for fear of retaliation from the gnomes. There
are also dreams received in childhood that the dreamer does not understand
until later. It took Jung many decades to understand a dream he had when
he was three and half years old. The dream portrayed a ritual phallus placed

on a golden throne in an underground chamber. This dream helped form the basis for the development of Jung's thought in the second half of his life.

Finally, there are night fears that are confronted only when the individual has attained the necessary inner freedom. It is only at the age of thirty that a musician decided to confront the sensation of a presence in his bedroom at night that had come to him on different occasions throughout his life from the time of childhood. As a child he recalled staying immobile, hiding under his blankets, paralyzed with fear. When as an adult he decided for the first time to relax and surrender to the experience, and to confront the dark closet associated with his fear, waves of energy ran through his whole body and the fear that had haunted him for many years gave way to a vision of light.

Appendix

The Evolving Theory and Research on Children's Dreams

Modern research on children's dreams began at the turn of the century. Since that time theorists have articulated several distinct points of view on children's dreams. Clinicians have used dreams in their therapeutic work with children. Cognitive psychologists have been interested in the comprehension of the dream concept by children of different ages. Researchers have explored the beginnings of dreaming in the life of the child and studied the contents of dreams of children at different ages, socioeconomic milieus, and levels of intelligence in both sexes.

Freud, Jung, and Piaget on Children's Dreams

In the West, dream research begins with the discovery of the unconscious and Sigmund Freud's first statements on this discovery in 1900. Although Freud himself devoted only a small proportion of his work to the dreams of children, and saw those dreams initially as nothing but wish fulfillment, his psychoanalytic theory, which emphasizes the repression of infantile sexuality, has nevertheless inspired the clinical approach of many child analysts, among them Susan Isaacs, Melanie Klein, and Anna Freud. And Freud's initial theory has led to some research centered on the contents of children's dreams.

Freud distinguished between the manifest content of the dream, which is the symbolic form with which the dream shows itself, and the latent content of the dream, which is concealed and skillfully disguised by the dream work performed upon it by the unconscious. Thus in its imaged form as the

121

manifest content, the dream for Freud has a deceptive appearance that hides from consciousness the real meaning of the dream, which can be revealed by interpretation.

Freud (1915) considered that in children the manifest and the latent content of the dream were confounded. For him, all children's dreams amounted to the fulfillment of wishes vividly experienced during the day. For example, eating cherries one has wanted to eat in waking life, climbing a mountain one had expected to climb the day before, or desiring to "grow up" or "live in the heroic times" of ancient Greece "riding in a chariot with Achilles, with Diomed as charioteer" (110, 111), all fulfill wishes.

Although Freud recognized that children's dreams could reveal some level of complexity and refinement, his interpretation nevertheless remained the same: "The dreams of little children are simple fulfillments of wishes, and as compared, therefore, with the dreams of adults, are not at all interesting. They present no problem to be solved, but are naturally invaluable as affording proof that the dream in its essence signifies the fulfillment of a wish" (1915, 107). Later, Freud modified the absolute character of his point of view, acknowledging a particularly elaborate and rich quality in the dreams of children who are four and five years old.

Jung (1960) found that children's dreams contained much of potential for the developing person. For Jung, childhood is a time for receiving "big dreams," dreams from a deeper layer of the unconscious that refer to the person's destiny in life: "Childhood, therefore, is important not only because various warpings of instincts have their origins there, but because this is the time when, terrifying or encouraging, these farseeing dreams and images appear before the soul of the child, shaping his whole destiny" (52).

The period between ages three and five corresponds to one of those crucial phases signaling the unfolding course of life, as do the periods of adolescence, the middle of life, and the approach of death. These periods of transition are often accompanied by big dreams characteristic of the "individuation process." Jung (1962) was astonished by the depth of certain dreams of children, "which are simply fabulous, so that one is astonished and 'tears one's hair' wondering how it is possible that a child can dream these things of which he has never heard" (308; translated by the author).

Jung considered Freud's sexual interpretation of dreams far too restrictive. For Jung, dreams are creations from the unconscious that express in the clearest and most economical way the present state of the dreamer's inner life. Often dreams compensate for the dreamer's conscious attitudes, thus functioning as a self-regulatory mechanism of psychic life. Dreams also have a prognostic function. In the decisive hours of life, they might indicate to the dreamer the way to follow or the orientation to make.

One of Jung's most original contributions to the theory of dreams has been his evidence for a collective unconscious, a layer of the psyche deeper than the personal unconscious, where symbolic forms transcend the strictly personal life of the dreamer and reach universal contents of our common psychological heritage. Jung has thus enlarged the prevailing conception of the legacy of the human psyche. His evidence for the collective unconscious has led him to say that the child's psyche is of infinite extent and incalculable age (Jung 1970).

Jean Piaget was interested in children's dreams insofar as dreams are a manifestation of symbolic thinking. He established a parallel between a child's play and a child's dreaming, and he applied his theory of play symbolism to dreams and to unconscious symbolism. Piaget (1962) criticized Freud's view that symbolic thought in dreams acts as a mechanism for camouflaging their true meanings. For Piaget, unconscious symbolism expresses more than what is suppressed or repressed. Piaget suggested that symbolism as found in dreams shows one of the pursuits of consciousness rather than a mechanism of camouflage. He conceived symbolic activity as the beginning of conscious assimilation, an attempt at understanding. Dreams are an extreme form of symbolic thought, but they abide by the same laws as other forms of thought:

> Symbolic thought is then the only possibility of awareness of the assimilation which takes place in affective schemas. This awareness is incomplete, and therefore distorting, since by the very nature of the situation the mechanisms which symbolic thought expresses are incapable of accommodation. It is, however, only awareness and not disguise. . . .
>
> On the whole, unconscious symbolic thought follows the same laws as thought in general, of which it is merely an extreme form, being an extension of symbolic play in the direction of pure assimilation. (209, 212)

Piaget (1962) showed that in its structure as well as its content, the child's dream appears to be a very close neighbor to the child's make-believe. In both, Piaget observed the same forms of subordinate symbolism tied to the body (suction, urination, excretion), to basic feelings about the family (love, jealousy, aggression), and to preoccupations centered on the birth of babies.

Piaget's theory furnishes a rigorous theoretical foundation outside the clinical tradition. Piaget established a basis for conceiving of the symbolic function in developmental terms, showing how it helps in adaptation. Piaget's perspective makes possible the insight that the process of dreaming "not only gives expression to particular kinds of content but at the same time restructures them in developmental terms" (Castle 1971, 109).

Neither Freud nor Jung made children's dreams a specific object of study. But both formulated basic positions on children's dreams that were later modified. Freud's reductionistic perspective, accounting for children's dreams as simple wish fulfillment, has proved too restrictive. Jung's point of view, however, which recognized the amplitude and potential of children's dreams, focused mainly on their archetypal dimension. Piaget, for his part, approached children's dreams as an active form of thought.

Between the simple wish-fulfillment dreams observed by Freud and the archetypal big dreams that Jung emphasized lies the universe of children's dreams that clinicians and researchers later explored. To Freud's and Jung's psychoanalytical and depth-analytic theories, Piaget's cognitive theory added a third term, one that completed the theoretical frame upon which later thought and research on children's dreams was hung.

Child Analysts' Concepts and Uses of Dreams

To this day the clinicians who are best known for their work with children's dreams remain Melanie Klein, Anna Freud, and Frances G. Wickes. To their work more recent clinicians promoting special emphasis on a developmental approach have contributed. Melanie Klein suggested that the first manifestations of nocturnal fears in children could be related to the main variety of anxiety that children will cope with during the rest of their lives. If children could be treated when these first anxieties show, Klein proposed, perhaps a neurosis could be caught at its onset and its development interrupted.

Klein (1963) perceived latent signs of guilt in the simple wish dreams of young children, and she urged psychoanalysts not to fear communicating depth interpretations that could soothe the anxiety of children in analysis: "My analysis of very young children's dreams in general has shown me that in them, no less than in play, there are always present not only wishes but counter-tendencies coming from the super-ego, and that even in the simplest wish-dreams the sense of guilt is operative in a latent way" (34n). Klein (1963) favored depth interpretations even at the beginning of analysis with children, since she saw psychological material in children returning again and again to consciousness, to be known and elaborated. She understood depth interpretation in analytical work with children as having the goal of encouraging unconscious material to surface and thus soothing the anxiety awakened by analytical work, and making way for the work of analysis.

Klein developed her technique of play analysis on the basis of Freud's teachings and way of working with dreams. She interpreted the elements in a child's play, including the content, the way of playing, the roles given to toys or taken on by the child, the motivations for abandoning or changing the kind of play, in the same manner that Freudians would interpret the elements of a dream. For Klein, dreams and play have a continuity between them, so that the dream of a child will be vivified and developed in the child's play.

Anna Freud (1974a) used nocturnal dreams, waking dreams, and drawings as technical aids in her analytical work with children. She observed that children in analysis dream no more and no less than adults, and that the dreams of children are not as simple as the examples quoted by Freud in his *Interpretation of Dreams* would lead us to believe: "We find in them the complicated distortions of wish fulfillment that correspond to the complicated neurotic organization of the child patient" (24).

In her analytic work, she brought the child to understand that the dream is not created out of nothing, but out of elements of the child's personal experience, and she invited the child to trace the origin of the dream with her: "At first account of a dream, I say, 'No dream can make itself out of nothing; it must have fetched every bit from somewhere'—and then I set off with the child in search of its origins. The child amuses himself with the pursuit of the individual dream elements as with a jigsaw puzzle, and with great satisfaction follows up the separate images or words of the dream into real life situations" (1974a, 25). At first enthusiastic about it, Anna Freud (1974b) later had to give up the method of free association with young children. She noticed that even if children spontaneously tell their dreams, they are neither disposed nor capable of engaging in free association, making dream interpretation with children "less fecund and less convincing" (6).

In *The Inner World of Childhood*, Frances G. Wickes (1978) drew on her experience as a child analyst to show how children encounter their inner world and use it. Wickes regarded the dream of the child with a particular attitude of respect and invited us "to treat the dream reverently as a gift that the child has given us" (237). By contrast to Klein, Wickes warned against the danger of prematurely interpreting the dreams of the child, and in so doing injuring "the mysterious process" of the dream and injuring the potential for transformation that the dream contains. She also referred to the danger of unduly turning the child's attention toward the world of the unconscious, which can lead the child to become too "self-conscious."

Wickes (1978) emphasized the importance of a child's quality of relationship with the inner world and with the world of the unconscious in general. She made a distinction between a fertile and creative relationship with the unconscious and a neurotic relationship in which fantasy beomes an escape from reality and a refusal to accept responsibility: "We must, even in our dealings with young children, keep clear the distinction between the fantasy which is creative and has the value that we find in poetry and works of imagination, and the fantasy which is used as a retreat from reality. Looking on the bright side by refusing to acknowledge existing conditions is another form of refusing responsibility" (192). The true value of the dream, in Wickes's view, resides in the link it provides with the conscious life of the dreamer and its relationship to the problems confronting the child at a given time.

Wickes's conception of the child's unconscious takes its inspiration from Jung. Just as an embryo and a mother share a common metabolism, so a young child shares a common state of psychic identity with a mother and, later, with both parents. This psychic identity is most of all a connection between the child's and the parents' unconscious. The unresolved and unconcious problems of the parents might be intuited by the child and expressed in the child's dream life. Wickes considered that such dreams then belong to the parents and must be approached with the parents.

In contrast to what Jung suggested, Wickes (1978) noted that "the cosmic dream, or the dream of the moon and stars, or the embodiment of the great forces of the universe" (262) may occur, but are far from being common in children. Fordham (1969), another follower of Jung, noted that archetypal motifs are active in childhood and that the anima, the animus, the shadow, and representations of the Self can be observed in dreams long before adolescence.

Among more recent clinical contributions to the freeing of interpretations of children's dreams, those of Rudolph Ekstein, Steven Luria Ablon and John E. Mack, Pierre Daco, and Maurice R. Green favor a cognitive and developmental approach. More and more, observed Ekstein (1981), analysts use dreams to further the therapeutic dialogue with the child, and they are prudent with their interpretation of the symbolic meanings of children's dreams. In his therapeutic work, Ekstein often approaches a dream in the manner of a fairy tale that describes a conflict and at the same time contains a method of adaptation.

From Ablon and Mack's (1980) point of view, children's dreams describe in imaged form their most pressing tasks and preoccupations at different phases in their development. Ablon and Mack suggested envisioning the dreaming of children "as a versatile and symbolically rich dimension of mental life through which the child can give creative and highly condensed metaphoric expression to the central dilemmas of his current existence" (188).

Daco (1979) emphasized the value of paying attention to children's dreams. He warned against "psychologism" (a "psychologistic attitude" that reduces the child as a human being instead of opening toward the child's own dimensions and experience). Green (1971) also conceived of dreaming as a resource of the child's imagination. He urged that "the manifest content be treated seriously as a language in its own right and not be dismissed as a mere superficial disguise or a secret code for underlying latent content" (75).

The attitude of child analysts with regard to dream interpretation with children has grown through the years. Whereas Melanie Klein considered it to be significant to interpret children's dreams and to communicate interpretations to them to allay anxiety, Frances G. Wickes warned against premature interpretations that run the risk of perturbing a psychic process at work in the child. And more recent analysts are prudent about symbolic interpretations of children's dreams and more inclined to conceive of dreaming as a resource of the imagination.

At first the dreams of children were used by practitioners of psychoanalysis for analytical and therapeutic purposes and for theory that supported the idea of dreams as revealers of neurotic symptoms. Gradually over the years, the interpretive approach was freed from this narrow task, and dreams could be taken for themselves. Child analysts recognized not only the therapeutic potential of dreams but also their creative value for the child's healthy development.

Genesis of the Child's Notion of Dreams

From a perspective completely different from that of child analysts, Jean Piaget as early as 1926 was interested in the notions children have of dreams. Piaget tried to discover how a child conceives of the dream phenomenon, its origin, and its location. Other questions he pursued concerned the organ the child supposed we dream with, the substance of dreams, their cause, and their realism. What do we dream with? What is a dream made of? Why do we dream? Are dreams real?

From the answers provided by children, Piaget (1979) identified three stages. Monique Laurendeau and Adrien Pinard (1962) repeated and standardized Piaget's study. Their observations confirmed and elaborated Piaget's findings. At stage 1 (four years old),[1] a child conceives of a dream as a phenomenon originating from a source external to the dreamer: "from the window," "from the moon," "from the night," and occurring outside the dreamer, say, in the dreamer's bedroom. The child sometimes believes that the dream is made with paper, with lead, or with sugar, and the child holds the dream to be true and objective.

Then the child enters a transitory phase that will take him or her from a "realist" to a "subjective" conception of the dream. At stage 2A (five years old), the interiorization of the conception of dreams begins, but on the whole the thinking of children at this stage remains very close to their thinking at the previous one. At stage 2B (five years and five months old), the child grasps the internal character either of the origin of the dream or of its location, but not of both.[2] It sometimes also happens that the child oscillates between an internal and an external conception of these two dimensions. Such a child might affirm, for instance, that the dream takes place "on the bedroom window" or "in the bedroom," and state at the same time that the dream is invisible to others because it takes place "in the head" or "in the eyes."

The children at stage 2C (six years old) understand the internal character of the dream phenomenon. They admit, however, that if a person opened the head of someone at the time she or he is dreaming, the person could see the dream inside. This reveals how a child at this stage retains a belief in the material existence of the dream. Beyond this phase of transition, children access a subjective notion of dreams. They have the notions that dreams are individual, internal, invisible, and immaterial.

Some children of stage 3 still have recourse to phenomenistic, artificialistic, moralistic, or finalistic arguments when they try to explain the cause of dreams: "It is God who permits it," "It is to make us laugh." These children are grouped under stage 3A (six years old and five months). Those who show no traces of precausal thinking in their notions of dreams have reached stage 3B (nine years and seven months old).

Piaget has shown how the notion of the dream evolves in the child through a series of stages, and his method involved asking simple questions. Without doubt, the basic scheme described by Piaget applies, although subsequent research brought out subtle differences based on religious education and on the modes of expression used, whether verbal or pictorial, for answering the experimenter's questions. Thus Hasidic Jewish children, whose religious teaching attributes to God the origins of dreams, show particular difficulties when faced with the question of the origin of dreams, whereas they understand the immaterial nature of dreams very well (Kahana 1970). And children age three to six draw the location of their dreams within or close to their bodies—in the belly, the head, the eyes, or in a cartoon bubble nearby—and this is not a rare phenomenon (Lurçat 1977).

The Beginnings of Dreaming in the Life of the Child

The discoveries of the last decades about sleep cycles, and rapid-eye-movement (REM) sleep in particular, raise the question of the beginnings of dreaming in the life of the child from new points of view. In 1937 Davis and Loomis (see Huon 1972) observed that the electrical activity of the adult brain, measured by an electroencephalograph (EEG), gave different readings according to the depth of sleep. They identified four stages of sleep, from the onset of sleep (stage I) to the deepest sleep (stage IV). Later, in 1953, Aserinsky and Kleitman (1955a, 1955b), following Aserinsky's observation that infants move their eyes while they sleep, combined EEG measurements with a device that measures movements of the eyes. They matched stages of adult sleep with eye movements and discovered rapid eye movements in stage I sleep. In 1955 Dement and Kleitman (1957) focused on REM sleep and discovered the connection between dreaming and REM sleep, which led to an objective method for detecting the occurrence of dreams.

REM sleep is closely related to oneiric activity. It is during the REM phases of sleep that, in fact, oneiric activity is most plentiful. The child experiences

REM sleep from the time of birth and even before, if we refer to Howard P. Roffwarg, Joseph N. Muzio, and William C. Dement's (1966) observations of children born prematurely. These authors' observations of premature infants suggest that an infant born prematurely at thirty weeks spends 80 percent of her or his total sleep in REM sleep. This percentage goes down to 67 percent between thirty and thirty-five weeks, and reaches 58 percent at thirty-six weeks. In the newborn infant one to fifteen days old (Roffwarg et al. 1964), the average for REM sleep is 60 percent of total sleep; between fourteen and twenty weeks old, the average declines to 40 percent; at one year old it is 30 percent; at three years old it falls to 20 percent, which is the average percentage in the adult.

The high proportion of REM sleep in the life of the newborn has led to speculation on the beginnings of dreaming in the life of children. Researchers have wondered whether oneiric activity could exist before the appearance of the symbolic function in the infant's development.

Howard P. Roffwarg, William C. Dement, and Charles Fisher (1964) supposed that what goes on in the newborn's mind during sleep is closely linked with what goes on in the infant's mind when the infant is awake, and that as perception and memory develop, oneiric activity develops parallel to it. It is possible, according to these authors, that before the acquisition of visual perception and visual memory, oneiric activity takes other forms, such as olfactory, gustatory, tactile, and kinesthetic forms.

Louis Breger (1967) suggested that REM sleep in the young child is a state of internal perceptual activity. He supposed that this state, which he called "proto-oneiric," serves to assimilate information received from the external world and to "consolidate" the developing structures of perception and memory. The fact that these structures are relatively undeveloped at birth, and the necessity to develop them, could account, according to Breger, for the high proportion of REM sleep in the newborn and in the first months of life.

Many researchers have maintained that dreaming in children could be traced back to the first year of life. A child's dreaming before the appearance of language is then inferred from the child's behavior during sleep: cries, smiles, and movements. H. von Hug-Hellmuth (1919) quotes the case of a child less than one year old who, having spent a day in the country playing at splashing water, reproduced similar splashing motions in his sleep at night. M.H. Erickson (1941) observed during the sleep of an eight-month-old girl an activity in dreams that resembled the play activity she had previously enjoyed with her father, then absent, before the evening meal.

By contrast to the adult, in whom there is a general reduction of the muscular tonus during the REM phases (even if many small muscular contractions are observed during this REM sleep of the adult), in children there is a noticeably higher frequency of small movements such as fluttering of the eyelids, rapid movements of the eyeballs, larger movements of the limbs, vocalizations, and irregular breathing. These muscular movements in children begin sometimes ten minutes before the onset of the REM phase and seem to diminish toward the end of this period. Thus the REM phase of sleep in young children is often called "agitated sleep" or the "active phase of sleep." Very intense in the first weeks, these bodily movements will continue for considerable periods of time in sleep until adolescence. These observations on the "agitated sleep" in young children echo earlier clinical observations by von Hug-Hellmuth and by Erikson of the child's dreaming and gestures during sleep.

The appearance of language leaves no doubt as to the presence of oneiric activity in very young children. The literature on dreams provides a set of examples of verbal manifestations of dreaming in children less than two years old. Susan Isaacs (1932) reported the case of a fourteen-month-old child who had awakened frightened saying that a rabbit was about to bite her. Selma H. Fraiberg (1950) referred to the dream of a fifteen-month-old boy who during his sleep yelled, "Let me down, let me down" (286). He had been tied to the examination table at the doctor's that day. John E. Mack (1965) referred to the nightmare of a child of thirteen months, during which he yelled, "Boom boom," which is what he had usually yelled at the sight of a vacuum cleaner. Piaget (1962) first observed dreams in children between twenty-one months and two years old.

The question of the nature and the function of REM sleep at the beginning of life remains open to the most creative speculations and brings with it the problem of the origin of consciousness itself.

The Contents of Children's Dreams

The study of the content of children's dreams has been the basis for the largest amount of research on children's dreams. Researchers have studied the content of the dreams of children of different ages, socioeconomic milieus, and intellectual levels of both sexes. Some of these studies are clinical, and others are exploratory. The most recent are laboratory studies.

Clinical Research

The three clinical studies presented here involve very young children, age one to six. In comparison with the exploratory studies in which the data have generally been collected in a single interview with each of many hundreds of subjects, clinical research has involved smaller groups of children and the data have been gathered over many interviews with the same subjects.

Ruth Griffiths (1970) conducted an original study on the imaginative life of children. She postulated that there exist different levels of thinking, of which dreaming is the first. It is in dreaming that the attention is most diffuse, but in dreaming the mind is nonetheless active. Waking dreams and other activities of the imagination in waking life come midway between dreaming and the logical thinking in which conscious functioning and contact with reality are highest.

Griffiths had a dynamic conception of dreams. For her, the dream content reflects not only the present experience but also the problems that require resolution in the future. The awareness of these problems is first elaborated in the form of fantasies. It is only later that they will show up in conscious thought and in action. To access the child's fantasies, Griffiths used different means, including drawing, having the child tell a story, mental imagery, a projective game, and dreams.

Griffiths's research method was characterized by a "policy of waiting." She believed that children's dreams and thoughts could only be observed over time and that any pressure imposed on children by continual questioning would only betray the phenomenon studied.

Griffiths worked with five-year-old children attending preschool. Thirty of these children came from a poor area of London. The twenty others were from Brisbane, Australia. They also came from a modest area, but the rural surroundings of Brisbane and the proximity to nature that it affords made it a more privileged milieu. The children from Brisbane reported an average of 0.78 dreams per interview, and those of London, 0.55 dreams. Among the children of London, four reported no dreams. With the children of Brisbane, all the children reported dreams, and most of them reported their dreams promptly. As for the quality of dreams, there was no significant difference between the two groups.

Griffiths showed that the same "pattern" shapes dreams, images, games, and ideas of children, and that dreams that reflect the problems and dynamics active in the lives of children form a continuity with the problems and dynamics expressed in other symbolic activities.

Louise J. Despert (1949) conceived of a form of interview through play that accesses the dreams of children. During individual sessions of play, she introduced the question of dreams by asking the child who plays with dolls or identifies with different story characters, "Do these people dream?" Then she changed the questions so that they apply to the child: "And you? Do you dream?" In some cases, she did not apply the questions to the child, but rather conducted the whole interview with questions about the experience of the fictional characters. Despert assumed that children attribute their own dream material to the dolls.

As well as using these individual sessions to acquire dreams from children, Despert gathered data from observing children's daily behavior. She noted spontaneous conversations between children about dreams or dream accounts following storytelling. Other information came from parents. But the individual play sessions remained the most significant source of Despert's data on children's dreams. She collected 190 dreams from 39 children aged two to five.

There was a great diversity among children in their ability to report dreams. In Despert's study one child reported thirty dreams. The accounts of dreams from the five-year-old children seemed the most reliable, for Despert could distinguish with certainty among dream, fantasy, and play experience. Despert's data on dream contents 'was classed in three categories: human beings, animals, and objects. Human characters and animals clearly predominated. Parents appeared in benevolent roles. But Despert noted that children quickly identify parents with powerful animal figures. Dream animals, generally enormous and terrifying, pursue the children, trying to bite them or devour them. But small animals that are not threatening in reality also play the role of threatening figures in the dreams of children.

Louise Bates Ames (1964) followed from fifty to one-hundred children from birth to the age of sixteen. She noted that the subjects of children's dreams change from one year to the next, according to a definite sequence. This sequence follows the fears children have. The object of fear in the child's waking life will show up in the child's dreams a year or so later. At two, children dream especially of trains. At three, they occasionally report dreams portraying their parents, their daily games, and farm animals. From four on, according to Ames, dream reports are more reliable. These dreams are of animals, and of wolves in particular.

Ames found that nightmares appear generally between the ages of five and seven, and again between ten and twelve. At five, the child is frequently awakened by a nightmare. Most often, these nightmares involve animals such as wolves or bears, which chase or bite, or strange and threatening characters, or events related to the elements fire and water, or fights. Children of this age also dream of objects in their bed and of domestic animals, especially dogs. At six, children dream of domestic animals, war, fire, thunder and lightning, personal difficulties, and objects in their room. At five and six, pleasant dreams refer to daily events and play, and to people familiar from the child's surroundings.

Clinical studies show great ingenuity in the methods used for accessing children's dreams. Despert's play interview has an imaginative quality, even if we may question her assumption that the dreams attributed by children to fictional characters reflect their own dreams. Griffiths's policy of waiting seeks to implement an attitude toward the dreams of children that respects them. Clinical studies have attested to the reliability of children's dream reports starting from age four and five, and have established what may be expected from both the recall and the contents of young children's dreams.

Exploratory Research

The first exploratory research on the content of children's dreams was marked by the influence of Freudian ideas about repressed infantile sexuality, a desire for the death of parents, and anxiety, wishes, and fears. This research was usually conducted through the schools but occasionally through the health clinics. It involved subjects from age one to eighteen.[3]

C. W. Kimmins's research (1973) during 1918–19, when he was chief inspector of schools in London, was the first and most elaborate of the genre. He collected a considerable number of dreams—fifty-nine hundred—with the help of teachers and children under his jurisdiction, from a population of children ranging in age from five to sixteen. Children from five to seven told their dreams individually to an observer, who transcribed the account. Starting from age eight, the children wrote down their dreams themselves.

Kimmins classified the contents of the dreams in general categories: wish fulfillment, fears, kinesthetic dreams, references to fairy tales, compensatory dreams, dreams of bravery and adventure, school activities, the influence of movies on dreams, the influence of stimulating books, death themes, and dreams in which conversations occurred.

In children of five to seven, 15 percent of the dreams were of wish fulfill-ment and 25 percent were of fears. These showed wild animals, older males, and especially, at age seven, robbers. Only 1 percent of the dreams referred to school activities, and these involved playground activities. Fairy-tale dreams were common among girls and less frequent among boys. The influence of movies was weak among girls but an important factor in boys of seven.

Between five and seven, the child was the center of her or his dream. The child of that age was rarely a passive observer. At seven, the dreams showed the presence of the family. According to Kimmins, death appeared in the dreams of the neurotic children. Dreams of bravery and adventure were rare among younger subjects. Sometimes the children imagined themselves tak-ing the form of objects or imagined themselves becoming animals. Kinesthetic elements were uncommon until age ten.

Phyllis Blanchard (1926) wanted to know the frequency and nature of dreams of children of different ages and levels of intelligence. She observed that children reported more dreams after the age of six, and she found no rela-tionship between intelligence level and dream life. She classified children's dreams by thematic categories: parents, animals, fears, play activities, falling, robbers, death, other family members, supernatural beings, wealth, and diverse games.

Blanchard collected 315 dreams from 189 subjects aged eighteen or less. Dreams that involved parents were the most frequent (15 percent). Most often parents appeared in benevolent roles. Then, in order of frequency, came animal dreams (14 percent). In accordance with Freudian theory, Blanchard observed that the great majority of children's dreams were either dreams of wish fulfillment (46 percent) or fear (40 percent). But very few of the dreams were of a sexual nature.

Josephine C. Foster and John E. Anderson (1936) studied the frequency of bad dreams in children and the factors that favor them. With the parents' collaboration, they collected dreams from children during seven consecutive days. Each morning the parents wrote a report describing the activities of the preceding night. As they grew older, children gradually had fewer bad dreams. Children were more likely to have bad dreams if they shared their bed or were in the bedroom with someone else, and specifically if this other person was an adult. Between one and four, children dreamed of animals. Between five and nine, bad dreams centered on strangers and bad guys, and children also dreamed of war, fire, and electricity. Between nine and twelve, bad dreams were linked to difficulties with friends and pet animals.

The better the health of the child, the less frequent the bad dreams. The dream content was usually influenced by the events of the preceding day, and also by such conditions as overexcitement, fatigue, sickness, indigestion, fear, worry, anger, and fighting.

Dreams, fears, wishes, tastes, and pleasant and unpleasant memories in children age five to thirteen were the object of a study by A. T. Jersild, F. V. Markey, and C. L. Jersild (1933). They found the same themes in the fears and dreams of children. Good dreams had themes of finding, acquiring, or receiving goods such as toys, money, food, clothes, and pet animals; traveling; enjoying themselves; and playing. Unpleasant dreams were about fires; the child falling, being pursued, being taken away or wounded; and about phantasmagorical beings. In children of five and six, there was a small percentage of dreams with magical events or phantasmagorical beings. Children with IQ's above 120 reported more unpleasant dreams than those of lower IQ measures.

In their study of seven hundred children in the first through sixth grades, Paul Witty and David Kopel (1939) noted that the incidence of dreams gradually diminished as children got older. Boys dreamed of accidents more often than girls, and of being physically injured or falling. Boys also reported more terrifying dreams with ghosts, mysterious phenomena, murders, and feelings of powerlessness than girls. Girls, by contrast, dreamed more frequently of benevolent fairies, magical phenomena, unfamiliar places and people, misfortunes befalling their parents or others, and of being pursued or threatened.

Beverly M. Elkan's (1969) more recent observations of the content of boys' dreams followed those of earlier researchers. Boys of four and five had monster dreams and dreams related to the fear of physical injury. Boys of eight and nine dreamed of events of community interest, goal-oriented tasks, projects of cooperation. The dreams of children of fourteen and fifteen revealed an interest in political and religious ideologies and preoccupations with their physical appearance.

In all this exploratory research, the children studied numbered in the hundreds. In most of the studies, the dreams were collected over a short period of time, often with a single interview or over a few days. In addition to the interview, a report of the dream written by the child from age eight (Kimmins 1973) and the report written by the child's parents (Foster and Anderson 1936) were used to collect dreams.

Researchers focused principally on the content of children's dreams. The other aspects considered were the relation between intelligence and dream life (Blanchard 1926; Jersild et al. 1933), differences in dream content between boys and girls (Kimmins 1973; Witty and Kopel 1939), the frequency of dream recall, the incidence of bad dreams, and the factors that led to them (Foster and Anderson 1936).

Researchers used a variety of systems of empirical classification. Categories referred to the predominant emotion in the dream such as fear, the function of the dream such as a compensatory dream, and the symbols in the dream. Sometimes a system of classification would go from one criterion to the other (Kimmins 1973; Blanchard 1926).

Laboratory Research

Laboratory research brought a new perspective to the content of children's dreams, insofar as it allowed access not only to those dreams that children are aware of and remember when awake but also to those they remain unconscious of.

David Foulkes (1978, 1979) showed that dreams spontaneously reported by children represent only a small percentage of the whole of their dream experience. Children are in REM sleep for periods ranging from ten to thirty minutes, four to six times a night. But they only rarely report dreams. Foulkes estimated that six- and seven-year-olds sleeping at home spontaneously report only one dream every 463 REM periods of sleep.

Laboratory research on children's dreams led Foulkes (1967, 1971; Foulkes et al. 1969) to conclude that the typical dream of the child is "simple and non-emotional." His young subjects, who were paid for their participation in his research, slept at the laboratory, where they were periodically awakened three to four times a night during REM phases and questioned about their dreams. Foulkes observed that the dreams of children are generally realistic in terms of the characters dreamed (parents, brothers, sisters, peers) and the sites and events referred to, and that they are relatively free of bizarre symbolism and unpleasant emotions and impulses.

The results of Foulkes's (1971) longitudinal study were that children of three and four reported dreams 27 percent of the time if they were awakened during REM sleep, 6 percent of the time if awakened during non-REM sleep, and 18 percent of the time if they were awakened at the onset of sleep.[4] In children of nine and ten, the recall during REM is 60 percent, 32 percent for non-REM, and 61 percent during sleep onset.

Using a coding system that he developed for children's dreams, Foulkes (1978, 1979, 1982) described the dream reports of children aged three and four as brief and relatively lacking in motor, emotional, and cognitive content. Foulkes's summary stated that action is reduced to a minimum in the dream of young children, and when it occurs, characters other than the children dreaming are the initiators of action. The theme of play was frequent in REM dreams of children aged three and four. The settings of the dreams are the child's house, the outdoors, and imprecise or vaguely described locations. What distinguished the dreams of three- and four-year-old children was the prominence of the animal theme. Parents, brothers, sisters, and peers were not present as often as farm animals or animals indigenous to the region.

Foulkes noted important changes in the accounts of children's dreams beginning when they are five and six. Dream reports doubled in length. And for the first time, almost all dreams took on the clear, although simple, aspect of a story. In their form, dreams more closely resembled adult dreams, and they were more dynamic than the dreams of three- and four-year-olds. The dreams of children at five and six contained members of their families, other familiar people, unknown characters who behaved in modes of familiar people, and animals whose species were directly known by the dreamers.

What is striking, noted Foulkes, was the passive role played by the dreamers in their dreams. The action that appeared in the dreams of five- and six-year-old children was attributed to characters other than the dreamers themselves. It was rare for dreamers to initiate hostile actions or be the object of them. The dream events were all related in some way to the children, but the children themselves were not directly involved. Foulkes noted more marked differences at five and six between the sexes than at any other age. Male strangers and indigenous animals occurred more often in the dreams of boys than of girls. There were more friendly interactions and happy outcomes in the dreams of girls.

At seven and eight, the dreamers had become active participants in their dreams. There was increasing activity and more numerous interactions. This was especially true for boys. The sexual differences diminished. The remaining differences unrelated to general aspects of dreaming were differences in content related to the development of gender roles. There were more female peers in girls' dreams than in boys' dreams, for example. From the age of seven and eight on, boys dreamed of family members and of known male peers rather than of animals. In boys' as well as girls' dreams, there was an increasing incidence of male strangers. In Foulkes's research, children of seven and eight reported dreams resembling those from older children and adults.

In a home laboratory using electrophysiological measures, Louis Breger (1969) found, in contrast to Foulkes, that with children from six to ten, dreams were often unpleasant and unrealistic. With the exception of conducting the research at home, his method was like that of Foulkes. The dreams that Breger collected included many scenes of aggression and physical woundedness, and the motif of death.

Laboratory research has had the value of showing the kind of dream images that usually occupy the child's mind while asleep. It has objectified many observations of earlier researchers, for example, the presence of the animal theme in the dreams of children age three to six, the significant change occurring in children's accounts of their dreams starting from age five to six, and the higher incidence of challenge dreams of boys than of girls.

From Freud to Jung to Piaget, from the consulting rooms of child analysts to the research laboratory, children's dreams have been the object of diverse scientific observation and speculation. This observation and speculation has concerned the origins of dreaming in the life of the child, the genesis of the notion of dreams in children, and most of all, the contents of children's dreams.

The evolving research into the dream life of children has begun to show the breadth and complexity that leads to valuing the place of dreams in the lives of children. But what is just beginning is the work of uncovering and knowing the reality of dreams, their monsters, and their profound stimulus for self-knowledge as children know them. In some small way the work that is just beginning may also permit children to come closer to what Frances G. Wickes (1978) referred to in 1927 as "that precious material" which is the stuff of poetry.

Notes

Introduction

1. The Senoi are divided into two groups, the Semais and the Temiars. Noone's study focuses on the Temiars.

2. In a lecture presented to the anthropology department of Cambridge University in 1934, titled "The Dream Psychology of the Senoi Shaman," Noone described the conception and practice of dreaming among the Senoi. In his book *In Search of the Dream People* (1972), Richard Noone, the anthropologist's brother, gave an account of this lecture. The American psychologist Kilton Stewart (1951), who joined Noone's team in Malaysia, also discussed the Senoi conception and practice of dreaming. The subject has been reviewed by another American psychologist, Patricia Garfield (1976), in *Creative Dreaming*.

3. It is not clear from the accounts of the Senoi culture the extent to which females undergo the same or similar education in dreaming as males. In consideration of the purposes this book serves, neutrality in identifying gender, except for the *halak*, has been practiced.

Chapter One: *Listening to the Dreamers*

1. Ruth Griffiths (1970), who conducted an original study on the imaginative life of children, found that "waiting" holds the possibility of yielding the best results in a study of young children: "A policy of waiting is found to yield the best results. We must not look for completed organised thoughts on every occasion that the child speaks, but be content with the scattered fragments he lets drop daily, believing that with time he will fill out the empty places and draw the frayed edges together. His thought develops bit by bit in relation to the medium of expression. To ask for more is often to demand what he does not yet possess. There would seem to be something almost of impertinence in an impatient forcing of a child's thought by continual questioning. If we are temporarily privileged to watch the gradual evolution of such a complex and delicate process as the thoughts of children, we must have regard for that law

of scientific method, which demands that the investigation shall in no way influence those phenomena to be observed. Psychology, like education, begins with respect for the child" (17). Griffiths's "policy of waiting" has been a source of inspiration for me. Griffiths combined the qualities of a clinician, an educator, and a researcher.

2. The population from which these children came lived in two sectors of the city of Ste.-Foy, both of them ,middle-class, with a mix of professional and white-collar workers with some blue-collar workers. *Canada Statistics* (1981) reported for the two sectors that, of those fifteen years old and above, 34 percent had college degrees and 66 percent had education up through technical schools; 46 percent in one sector and 42 percent in the other were professionals; 40 percent and 45 percent, respectively, were white-collar workers; 14 percent and 13 percent were blue-collar workers.

3. David Foulkes et al. (1969), who used the electrophysiological method, noted that dream reports given by children in laboratory contexts do not necessarily describe the real content of their dreams, particularly the dreams of preschool-age children. They speculated that this phenomenon is due to children's difficulty in conceptualizing or communicating, and possibly due to confabulation (see Ablon and Mack 1980). Children's dreams reported in Breger's (1969) electrophysiological research conducted at home yield a strong impression of the same confabulatory quality. The child's account often began with the formula "Once upon a time . . ." and resembled typical children's confabulations and waking fantasies, with magical elements, metamorphoses, and other fictional forms.

4. For the design of the interview, I was inspired by the works of Leon J. Yarrow (1960), John Rich (1968), and Jerome L. Singer (1973), which addressed the issues of interviewing children for the purpose of research. I also drew from my practice of "l'interrogatoire clinique," or clinical interview, as developed by Piaget (1979) for the study of thought processes of children.

5. In poetic language, Frances G. Wickes (1978) captures some of the essential attitudes of a fertile relationship with a child: "We learn to think of a child as a tree planted besides the rivers of water, that brings forth its fruit in its season. We wait for that deep relationship which is our only way of discovering the real depths of a child's nature; of another human being we can have only that part which is revealed to us in love" (58).

Chapter Two: *What Boys and Girls Dream About*

1. One male child's dream reports were not retained for this compilation because of their highly confabulatory character and considerable length. Classifying his dream reports with the other dreams ran the risk of following an obviously too arbitrary criterion.

2. We speak of dreams as if the dream experience were one, but in fact the experience is one of infinite diversity. First, we dream at different levels of consciousness and our dreams themselves are at different levels. A continuum might very likely be established going from the dim and indistinct dreams of drowsy sleep to the most vivid dreams, which call forth higher levels of lucidity from the dreamers. Second, we generally associate dreams with sleeping. But beyond the dream of the one who sleeps there is the dream of the one who is awake. The involuntary visual activity occurring

during a dream may be the same activity occurring during meditation, hypnosis, isolation, fasting, and the practices of incubation and certain rituals.

Most dream theorists and researchers have attempted to establish some kind of distinction between different dream experiences. For example, Freud distinguished among dreams by the stimuli that provoked them, like a full bladder or a repressed wish. He also distinguished among them by the amplitude of the "dream work" performed, and the extent of the gap between the "manifest," or apparent, and the "latent," or underlying, contents of a dream. Jung spoke of "big dreams" and "ordinary dreams." He also took note of anticipatory dreams, which seemed to be about events that had not yet occurred. In the East in some yogic traditions, an even more differentiated conception of levels of dreaming and of dreams has been postulated. In these traditions there is held to be a hierarchy of bodies increasingly more subtle than the physical body, designated as the etheric, astral, mental, spiritual, cosmic, and nirvanic bodies. Each of these seven bodies gives access to a specific level of reality and to a distinct type of dream. And sometimes one dream comprises more than one of these levels. We still know little about how to discriminate the different oneiric experiences that we have, since we are only beginning to extend the frontiers of our consciousness and to explore the interior spaces that this expansion opens up for us.

3. Sonja Marjasch (1967) reminds us that the object of dream psychology can only be the remembered dream, not the immediate experience of the dreamer as she or he dreams: "A dream is first of all an individual experience of the subject, and the subject cannot at the moment of the experience share it with anyone else. Thus the dream as an immediate experience can never be the object of psychology. Dream psychology can only pay attention to the remembered dream" (128; translated by the author).

Then Marjasch describes the dream as a living reality that changes when told, when written down, and through time: "But we must keep in mind that dreams are not dead things as for example the broken pieces of a vase. In truth, there are inanimate dreams . . . But they cannot be used practically. Meanwhile, there are a large number of dreams that have as much life as fish out of water, which suffocate and writhe on the ground. Certain dreams are rather mobile, they change form. When told, intensities are modified, parts are added, and when put down in writing, certain dreams are curiously reduced to two thin lines, others extend to the narrator's astonishment over many pages. Certain dreams are remembered for a lifetime, others are forgotten in an instant" (128, 129; translated by the author).

Between the moment a dream is first lived and the moment it takes on its remembered form, the moment it is told, written down, or drawn, and the moment it is integrated into the dreamer's life and then forgotten, a long process has taken place. And at whatever moment we collect a dream, it is always at a given point along a curve of continuous change.

The phenomenon of dream alteration observed at an individual level shows up in another form in collective symbolism. The collective representations that constitute the symbolism of any religion are likely to have their origin in individual experiences, dreams, and visions that have since been expurgated and aligned to prevailing religious traditions. According to von Franz (1980a), there are very few unedited accounts of the religious experience of saints, for example, including their visions. These were rarely published without first being purified of what was considered "personal material." In the same way, among American Indians certain details considered uninteresting from the point of view of traditional ideas were omitted from accounts of the individual experience of dreamers and from accounts of apprentice shamans.

4. The word *numinous* expresses the presence of a quality attributed to the gods—shining, powerful, partaking of unconscious light and energy. Rudolph Otto's *Idea of the Holy* describes it at great length.

Chapter Four: *Amplifying Children's Dream Series*

1. Jean Chevalier and Alain Gheerbrant (1973) have described the way their dictionary of symbols functions with regard to the nature of symbols:

> Given its objective, this dictionary cannot be a collection of definitions, like lexicons or ordinary vocabularies, since a symbol escapes all definition. By the very nature of its function the symbol breaks established frames and reunites extremes within a single vision. The symbol is like the arrow *which flies and which does not fly*, both immobile and fugitive, obvious and impossible to grasp. Words are indispensable for suggesting the meaning or the meanings of a symbol; but let us always remember that they are incapable of expressing all of their values. May the reader not mistake our brief formulas for capsules enclosing within their narrow limits all dimensions of a symbol. . . .
>
> The imaginative reader will find in these pages, to tell the truth, more stimulation than knowledge. . . .
>
> The different interpretations by which we have signified many symbols are certainly not without relationship among themselves, as harmonics are related to a fundamental tone. But the basic meaning is not always obvious and it may not be the same in every cultural area. This is why, most often, we have restricted ourselves to juxtaposing many interpretations, without attempting any reduction that would run the risk of being arbitrary. The reader should also suspend concreteness and follow his or her own intuition. (xii, xiii, xv; translated by the author)

2. Marie-Louise von Franz, from an unpublished 1979 speech titled "Meaning and Order," presented at the Pennarion Conference in Los Angeles.

Chapter Five: *The Combat with the Monster*

1. Von Franz (1977) observes that when a psychic content is too chaotic or too undifferentiated, it cannot be met directly but only indirectly by means of magic.

2. In French, "Jos Lit" is pronounced "Joe Lee" and literally means "Joe Bed."

Chapter Six: *The Taming of the Monster*

1. Originally the total number of dreams related by Pierre was twelve. One of them was a dream remembered from the past. For this part of the analysis of the dynamic evolution through a dream series, that dream has been excluded because it did not fit chronologically within the period in which the series was dreamed.

2. "Bug" is a translation of *bibite*, which can mean an insect of indeterminate type and also an indeterminate animal of small size.

3. "The symbolism of the Terrible Mother draws its image predominantly from the 'inside,' that is to say, the negative elementary character of the Feminine expresses itself in fantastic and chimerical images that do not originate in the outside world. The reason for this is that the Terrible Female is a symbol for the unconscious. And the dark side of the Terrible Mother takes the form of monsters, whether in Egypt or India, Mexico or Etruria, Bali or Rome. In the myths and tales of all peoples, ages and countries—even in the nightmares of our own nights—witches and vampires, ghouls and spectres, assail us, all terrifyingly alike" (Neumann 1972, 148).

4. *L'homme à la découverte de son âme* (Paris: Petite Bibliothèque Payot, 1962) is a collection of texts by Jung, some of which are also available in English. But chapter 8 from which I quote corresponds to part three of *Introduction à la psychologie analytique*, an untranslated text adapted by Roland Cahen from stenographed notes taken by an auditor and reviewed by Jung of a series of lectures presented in Basel at the "Société de Psychologie" in 1934.

5. According to Erik H. Erikson (1963), one of the characteristic conflicts of the five-year-old child is polarized between initiative on the one hand and guilt on the other, "over the goals contemplated and the acts initiated in one's exuberant enjoyment of new locomotor and mental power: acts of aggressive manipulation and coercion, which soon go far beyond the executive capacity of the organism and mind and therefore call for an energetic halt in one's contemplated initiative" (256).

6. Commenting on the thought of Jung, Erich Neumann (1970) says: "He shows, first, that the hero's fight is the fight with a mother who cannot be regarded as a personal figure in the family romance. Behind the personal figure of the mother there stands, as is evident from the symbology, what Jung was later to call the mother archetype. Jung was able to prove the transpersonal significance of the hero's fight because he did not make the personal family aspect of modern man the starting point of human development, but rather the development of the libido and its transformations" (153).

Chapter Seven: *The Engulfment by the Monster*

1. "The so-called Oedipus complex with its famous incest tendency changes at this level into a 'Jonah-and-the-Whale' complex, which has any number of variants, for instance the witch who eats children, the wolf, the ogre, the dragon, and so on. Fear of incest turns into fear of being devoured by the mother. The regressing libido apparently desexualizes itself by retreating back step by step to the presexual stage of earliest infancy. Even there it does not make a halt, but in a manner of speaking continues right back to the intra-uterine, pre-natal condition and, leaving the sphere of personal psychology altogether, irrupts into the collective psyche where Jonah saw the 'mysteries' ('représentations collectives') in the whale's belly. The libido thus reaches a kind of inchoate condition in which, like Theseus and Peirithous on their journey to the underworld, it may easily stick fast. But it can also tear itself loose from the maternal embrace and return to the surface with new possibilities of life" (Jung 1956, 419–20).

Encountering the Monster

2. "The symbolism of 'the center' embraces a number of different ideas: the point of intersection of the cosmic spheres (the channel joining hell and earth; . . . a place that is hierophanic and therefore *real*, a supremely 'creational' place, because the source of all reality and consequently of energy and life is to be found there" (Eliade 1963, 318).

Chapter Eight: *The Monster as Initiator*

1. The daemones are minor gods. The Romans called them *genii*. The daemones or demons are not pure spirits, but they have a subtle and light body. They are in the atmosphere that surrounds the earth, whereas the gods are up in the sky. We can attract their favors or we can provoke their anger (von Franz 1980).

2. " 'Religious dread' (or 'awe') would perhaps be a better designation. Its antecedent stage is 'daemonic dread' (cf. the horror of Pan) with its queer perversion, a sort of abortive offshoot, the 'dread of ghosts'. It first begins to stir in the feeling of something 'uncanny', 'eerie', or 'weird'. It is this feeling which, emerging in the mind of primeval man, forms the starting point for the entire religious development in history" (Otto 1958, 14).

3. "Promenons-nous dans le bois, tandis que le loup y est pas. Le loup y es-tu, entends-tu, gros bossu, nez pointu!" Et le loup de répondre: "Le loup met ses bottes, . . . Le loup met son manteau . . . son chapeau." This traditional children's game is played throughout the French-speaking world.

4. This is the French from which the author has translated:

Le cri de la Bête lui ouvre le poitrail
passage d'extrême consentement
issue déjà
Elle a reconnu l'espace
'l'enchantement profond'
où devenir captive sans mourir
puis souveraine sous la cicatrice d'aujourd'hui
la gorge du temps
soleil au fond du cloître . . .

Ainsi Elle est en la Bête
en suspension de vie et pourtant vivante
passagère d'une barque désormais instituable
désormais lieu acquiescement
et muqueuses de soie.

5. Verda Heisler, "The Relationship of Ego and Self in the Individuation Process," lecture presented to The Friends of Jung, San Diego, California, in 1981.

6. My observation contrasts markedly with that of Foulkes (1982), according to whom the main setting of a girl's dreams is inside the house, and the boy's is outside. His study shows that almost 50 percent of the dreams of girls between the ages of five and seven take place inside the house, compared to less than 25 percent of boys' dreams. In my study, 38.6 percent of boys' dreams took place inside the house, compared with 20.3 percent of girls'.

Chapter Nine: *Steps toward Oneiric Education*

1. Kilton Stewart, who studied the Senoi in 1936, observes at the end of his dissertation, later presented at the University of London, that the *tohats* (the highest-ranking dream workers) had begun to dream of ways to help the Temiar Senoi integrate their culture with the dominant Malay culture that surrounded them (Randall 1983).

2. In his account of his trip to the land of the Temiar Senoi in the Upper Perak of Malaysia in 1982 in search of the truth about the Temiar Senoi, Alexander Randall (1983) found that none of the young boys who acted as his guides and translators had received any training in dreaming or been part of a family discussion on dreams or heard about *halaks* or *tohats*. They had heard stories from their grandparents about dreams, but they had received no education in dreaming.

Appendix

1. The ages of access to the different stages are those found by Laurendeau and Pinard in their study with a population of five hundred Québécois children aged four to twelve, with fifty children in each age group.

2. Piaget believed that the child first discovers the internal character of the origin of dreams, then the location of the dream. Laurendeau and Pinard have shown that the sequences are varied. Shweder and LeVine (1975) have also shown the diversity in sequences followed by Hausa children in Niger.

3. See DeMartino 1959 for more information.

4. The partial results of this study have been published in different texts (Foulkes 1971, 1979). The study was published in its complete form in 1982.

References

Ablon, S. L., and J. E. Mack. 1980. "Children's Dreams Reconsidered." *Psychoanalytic Study of the Child* 35:179–217.

Aeppli, E. 1978. *Les rêves et leur interprétation* [Dreams and their interpretation]. Paris: Petite Bibliothèque Payot.

Ajuriaguerra, J. de. 1974. *Manuel de psychiâtrie de l'enfant* [Manual of child psychiatry]. Paris: Masson.

Ames, L. B. 1964. "Sleep and Dreams in Childhood." In E. Harms, ed., *Problems of Sleep and Dreams in Childhood* 6–29. International Series of Monographs on Child Psychiatry. New York: Pergamon Press.

Arnold-Forster, M. 1921. *Studies in Dreams.* London: Macmillan.

Aserinsky, E., and N. Kleitman. 1955a. "Two Types of Ocular Motility Occurring in Sleep." *Journal of Applied Physiology* 8:1–10.

———. 1955b. "A Motility Cycle in Sleeping Infants as Manifested by Ocular and Gross Body Activity." *Journal of Applied Physiology.* 8:11–18.

Barber, Y. C. 1978. *The Psychic Reality of Dreams.* New York: Exposition Press.

Blanchard, P. 1926. "A Study of Subject Matter and Motivation of Children's Dreams." *Journal of Abnormal Social Psychology* 21:24–37.

Breger, L. 1967. "Function of Dreams." *Journal of Abnormal Psychology Monograph* 72:1–28.

———. 1969. "Children's Dreams and Personality Development." In J. Fisher and L. Breger, eds., *The Meaning of Dreams: Recent Insight from the Laboratory*, 64–100. Sacramento, Calif.: Department of Mental Hygiene.

Campbell, J. 1949. *The Hero with a Thousand Faces.* New York: Pantheon Books.

———. 1964. *The Masks of God: Occidental Mythology.* New York: Viking Press.

147

Castle, P. W. 1971. "Contributions of Piaget to a Theory of Dreaming." In J. H. Masserman, ed., *Dream Dynamics: Scientific Proceedings of the American Academy of Psychoanalysis*, 99–116. New York: Grune-Stratton.

Chevalier, J. and A. Gheerbrant. 1973. *Dictionaire des symboles* [Dictionary of symbols]. Paris: Seghers et Jupiter. (Original work published 1969.)

Cirincione, D., J. Hart, W. Karle, and A. Switzer. 1980. "The Functional Approach to Using Dreams in Marital and Family Therapy." *Journal of Marital and Family Therapy*. (April):147–51.

Cirlot, J. E. 1962. *A Dictionary of Symbols*. Trans. Jack Sage. New York: Philosophical Library.

Daco, P. 1979. *L'interprétation des rêves* [The interpretation of dreams]. Verviers, Belgium: Marabout.

DeClerque, C. 1978. "Educating Children to Use Dreams." *Sundance* 2, no. 1:62–70.

DeMartino, M. F. 1959. "A Review of the Literature on Children's Dreams." In M. F. DeMartino, ed., *Dreams and Personality Dynamics* 87–96. Springfield, Ill.: Thomas Books.

Dement, W., and N. Kleitman. 1957. "The Relation of Eye Movement during Sleep to Dream Activity: An Objective Method for the Study of Dreaming." *Journal of Experimental Psychology* 53:339–46.

Despert, J. L. 1949. "Dreams in Children of Preschool Age." *Psychoanalytic Study of the Child* 3–4:141–80.

De Vries, A. 1974. *Dictionary of Symbols and Imagery*. Amsterdam: North-Holland.

Ekstein, R. 1981. "Some Thoughts Concerning the Clinical Use of Children's Dreams." *Bulletin of the Menninger Clinic* 45, no. 2:115–24.

Elkan, B. M. 1969. "Developmental Differences in the Manifest Content of Children's Reported Dreams." Ph.D. diss., University of Columbia.

Eliade, M. 1958. *Birth and Rebirth*. Trans. Willard R. Trask. New York: Harper Brothers.

———. 1960. *Myths, Dreams and Mysteries*. Trans. Philip Mairet. New York: Harper Brothers. (Original work published 1957.)

———. 1963. *Patterns in Comparative Religion*. Trans. Rosemary Sheed. New York: World Publishing.

Erickson, M. H. 1941. "On the Possible Occurrence of a Dream in an Eight-Month-Old Infant." *Psychoanalytic Quarterly* 10:382–84.

Erikson, E. H. 1959. "Identity and the Life Cycle." *Psychological Issues* 1, no. 1:1–171.

———. 1963. *Childhood and Society*. 2d rev. ed. New York: W. W. Norton.

Fordham, M. 1969. *Children as Individuals*. New York: Putnam.

Foster, J. C. and J. E. Anderson. 1936. "Unpleasant Dreams in Childhood." *Child Development* 7:77–84.

Foulkes, D. 1967. "Dreams of a Male Child: Four Case Studies." *Journal of Child Psychology and Psychiatry* 8:81–98.

_____. 1971. "Longitudinal Studies of Dreams in Children." In J. H. Masserman, ed., *Dream Dynamics: Scientific Proceedings of the American Academy of Psychoanalysis,* 48-71. New York: Grune-Stratton.

_____. 1978. "Dreams of Innocence." *Psychology Today* (December):78–88.

_____. 1979. "Children's Dreams." In B. B. Wolman, ed., *Handbook of Dreams,* 131–67. New York: Van Nostrand Reinhold.

_____. 1982. *Children's Dreams.* New York: Wiley.

Foulkes, D., J. D. Larson, E. M. Swanson, and M. Rardin. 1969. "Two Studies of Childhood Dreaming." *American Journal of Orthopsychiatry* 39:627–43.

Fraiberg, S. H. 1950. "Sleep Disturbances of Early Childhood." *Psychoanalytic Study of the Child* 5:285–309.

Freud, A. 1974a. "Introduction to Psychoanalysis." In *The Writings of Anna Freud.* Vol. 1, 1922–35. New York: International Universities Press.

_____. 1974b. "Indications for Child Analysis and Other Papers." In *The Writings of Anna Freud.* Vol. 4, 1945–56. New York: International Universities Press.

Freud, S. 1915. *The Interpretation of Dreams.* Trans. A. A. Brill. London: George Allen & Unwin. (Original work published 1900.)

Fromm, E. 1951. *The Forgotten Language.* New York: Holt, Rhinehart and Winston.

Garfield, P. 1976. *Creative Dreaming.* New York: Ballantine Books. (Original work published 1974.)

_____. 1984. *Your Child's Dreams.* New York: Ballantine Books.

Grant, M. and J. Hazel. 1981. *Dictionaire de la mythologie* [Dictionary of mythology]. Trans. Etienne Leyris. Verviers, Belgium: Marabout. (Abridged work based on *Who's Who in Classical Mythology,* London: Weidenfeld and Nicolson, 1973.)

Green, M. R. 1971. "Clinical Significance of Children's Dreams." In J. H. Masserman, ed., *Dream Dynamics: Scientific Proceedings of the American Academy of Psychoanalysis,* 72–94. New York: Grune-Stratton.

Griffiths, R. 1970. *A Study of Imagination in Early Childhood.* Westport, Conn.: Greenwood Press. (Original work published 1935.)

Hamilton, E. 1942. *Mythology.* Boston: Little, Brown.

Handler, L. 1972. "The Amelioration of Nightmares in Children." *Psychotherapy: Theory, Research and Practice* 9, no. 1:54–56.

Henderson, J. L. 1967. *Thresholds of Initiation*. Middleton, Conn.: Wesleyan University Press.

Hudson, J. O., and C. O'Connor. 1981. "The PEACE Process: A Modified Senoi Technique for Children's Nightmares." *School Counselor* 28, no. 5:347-52.

Huon, H. 1972. "Physiologie du sommeil de l'enfant [Physiology of children's sleep]." *Revue de neuropsychiatrie infantile et d'hygiène mental de l'enfance* 20:815-27.

I Ching or Book of Changes. 1967. Trans. Richard Wilhelm and Cary F. Baynes. Princeton: Princeton University Press. (Original work published 1950.)

Isaacs, S. 1932. *The Nursery Years*. New York: Vanguard Press.

Jacobi, J. 1971. *Complex, Archetype, Symbol*. Trans. Ralph Manheim. Princeton: Bollingen, Princeton University Press.

_____. 1973. *The Psychology of C. G. Jung*. Trans. Ralph Manheim. New Haven: Yale University Press.

Jaffé, A. 1964. "Symbolism in the Visual Arts." In C. G. Jung, *Man and His Symbols* 230-71. Garden City, N.Y.: Doubleday.

Jersild, A. T., F. V. Markey, and C. L. Jersild. 1933. "Children's Fears, Dreams, Wishes, Daydreams, Likes, Dislikes, Pleasant and Unpleasant Memories." *Child Development Monograph* 12. New York: Teacher's College, Columbia University.

Jones, R. M. 1971. "Discussion of Papers of David Foulkes, Ph.D., and Maurice R. Green, M.D." In J. H. Masserman, ed., *Dream Dynamics: Proceedings of the American Academy of Psychoanalysis*, 95-97. New York: Grune-Stratton.

Jung, C. G. 1953a. *Psychology and Alchemy*. Trans. R. F. C. Hull. Vol. 12 of *The Collected Works of C. G. Jung*. 20 vols. New York: Pantheon Books.

_____. 1953b. *Psychological Reflections*. London: Routledge and Kegan Paul.

_____. 1954. *The Practice of Psychotherapy*. Trans. R. F. C. Hull. Vol. 16 of *The Collected Works of C. G. Jung*. 20 vols. New York: Pantheon Books.

_____. 1956. *Symbols of Transformation*. Trans. R. F. C. Hull. Vol. 5 of *The Collected Works of C. G. Jung*. 20 vols. New York: Pantheon Books.

_____. 1960. *The Structure and Dynamics of the Psyche*. Trans. R. F. C. Hull. Vol. 8 of *The Collected Works of C. G. Jung*. 20 vols. New York: Pantheon Books.

_____. 1962. *L'homme à la découvrte de son âme* [Man discovering his soul]. Trans. Roland Cahen. Paris: Petite Bibliothèque Payot.

_____. 1965. *L'âme et la vie* [The soul and life]. Trans. Roland Cahen. Paris: Buchet-Chastel.

_____. 1967. *VII Sermones ad Mortuos* [Seven sermons to the dead]. London: Stuart and Watkins.

————. 1970. *The Development of Personality.* Trans. R. F. C. Hull. Vol. 17 of *The Collected Works of C. G. Jung.* 20 vols. Princeton: Princeton University Press.

————. 1972. *Mandala Symbolism.* Trans. R. F. C. Hull. Princeton: Bollingen, Princeton University Press.

Kahana, B. 1970. "Stages of the Dream Concept among Hasidic Children." *Journal of Genetic Psychology* 116:3–9.

Kalff, D. M. 1980. *Sandplay.* Trans. Wendayne Ackerman. Santa Monica, Calif.: Sigo Press.

Kellogg, R. 1969. *Analyzing Children's Art.* Palo Alto, Calif.: Mayfield.

Kimmins, C. W. 1973. "Children's Dreams." In S. G. M. Lee and A. R. Mayer, eds., *Dreams and Dreaming,* 83–109. Middlesex, England: Penguin. (Original work published 1931.)

Klein, M. 1963. *The Psycho-analysis of Children.* 3rd ed. Trans. Alix Strachey. London: Hogarth Press. (Original work published 1932.)

Koch, K. 1970. *Wishes, Lies, and Dreams.* New York: Vintage Books.

Laurendeau, M. and A. Pinard. 1962. *Causal Thinking in the Child.* New York: International Universities Press.

Lurçat, L. 1977. "Une approche de l'espace mentale [An approach to mental space]." *Journal de psychologie normale et pathologique* 74:431–49.

Mack, J. E. 1965. "Nightmares, Conflict and Ego Development in Childhood." *International Journal of Psycho-analysis* 46:403–28.

————. 1970. *Nightmares and Human Conflict.* Boston: Little, Brown.

Marjasch, S. 1967. "Sur la psychologie du rêve de C. G. Jung [On the dream psychology of C. G. Jung]." In R. Callois and G. E. von Grunebaum, *Le rêve et les sociétés humaines* [Dreaming and human society], 128–44. Paris: Gallimard.

Monneret, S. 1976. *Le sommeil et les rêves* [Sleep and dreams]. Paris: Retz.

Neumann, E. 1970. *The Origins and History of Consciousness.* Trans. R. F. C. Hull. Princeton: Bollingen, Princeton University Press. (Original work published 1954.)

————. 1972. *The Great Mother.* Trans. Ralph Manheim. Princeton: Bollingen, Princeton University Press. (Original work published 1955.)

————. 1973. *The Child.* Trans. Ralph Manheim. New York: C. G. Jung Foundation, Putnam.

Noone, R. 1972. *In Search of the Dream People.* New York: William Morrow.

Oriol-Boyer, C. 1975. "Les monstres de la mythologie grecque [The monsters of Greek mythology]." In *Le monstre 1, présence du monstre, mythe et réalité* [The monster 1: the presence of the monster, myth and reality], 25–50. Cahier de recherche sur l'imaginaire. Paris: Circé Lettres Modernes.

Otto, R. 1958. *The Idea of the Holy*. Trans. John W. Harvey. New York: Oxford University Press. (Original work published 1917.)

Perera, S. B. 1981. *Descent to the Goddess*. Toronto: Inner City Books.

Piaget, J. 1962. *Play, Dreams and Imitation in Childhood*. Trans. C. Gattegno and F. M. Hodgeson. London: Routledge and Kegan Paul. (Original work published 1946.)

———. 1979. *The Child's Conception of the World*. Trans. Joan and Andrew Tomlinson. Totowa, N.J.: Littlefield, Adams. (Original work published 1926.)

Randall 5th, A. 1983. "The Terrible Truth of the Temiar Senoi." *The Dream Network Bulletin* 2, no. 2:1–2.

Rich, J. 1968. *Interviewing Children and Adolescents*. New York: St. Martin's Press.

Roffwarg, H. D., W. C. Dement, and C. Fisher. 1964. "Preliminary Observations of the Sleep-Dream Pattern in Neonates, Infants, Children and Adults." In E. Harms, ed., *Problems of Sleep and Dreams in Childhood* 60–72. International Series of Monographs on Child Psychiatry. New York: Macmillan.

Roffwarg, H. D., J. N. Muzio, and W. C. Dement. 1966. "Ontogenic Development of the Human Sleep-Dream Cycle." *Science* 152:604–19.

Shweder, R. A. and R. A. LeVine. 1975. "Dream Concept of Hausa Children." *Ethos* 3, no. 2:209–30.

Singer, J. L. 1973. *The Child's World of Make-believe*. New York: Academic Press.

Stanton, J. 1982. *La nomade* [The nomad]. Montreal: L'Hexagone.

Stewart, K. 1951. "Dream Theory in Malaysia." *Complex* 6:21–33.

von Franz, M. L. 1964. "The Process of Individuation." In C. G. Jung, *Man and His Symbols*, 158–229. Garden City, N.Y.: Doubleday.

———. 1974. *Shadow and Evil in Fairytales*. Irving, Tex.: Spring Publications.

———. 1976. *The Feminine in Fairytales*. 2d rev. ed. Irving, Tex.: Spring Publications.

———. 1977. *Individuation in Fairytales*. New York: Spring Publications.

———. 1980a. *Alchemy*. Toronto: Inner City Books.

———. 1980b. *Redemption Motifs in Fairytales*. Toronto: Inner City Books.

———. 1980c. *Golden Ass*. 2d rev. ed. Irving, Tex.: Spring Publications.

von Hug-Hellmuth, H. 1919. *A Study of the Mental Life of the Child*. Trans. James J. Putman and Mabel Stevens. Washington, D.C.: Nervous and Mental Diseases Publishing Co.

Werlin, E. G. 1967. "An Experiment in Elementary Education. In R. M. Jones, ed., *Contemporary Educational Psychology*, 233–53. New York: Harper & Row.

Wickes, F. G. 1978. *The Inner World of Childhood*. Englewood Cliffs, N.J.: Prentice-Hall. (Original work published 1927.)

Witty, P., and D. Kopel. 1939. "The Dreams and Wishes of Elementary School Children." *Journal of Educational Psychology* 30:199–205.

Yarrow, L. J. 1960. "Interviewing Children." In P. H. Mussen, ed., *Handbook of Research Methods in Child Development*, 561–602. New York: Wiley.

Young, S. J. 1977. *Psychic Children*. New York: Pocket Books.

Index

155